V. R. Wilson was brought up in North Wales. She read History at Aberystwyth University and afterwards gained further qualifications through part time study. Her working career was short but varied. On moving back to North Wales, a caring role followed – parents, then husband! Membership of various public bodies has ensured she has had little opportunity to be idle.

RINGS OF GUILT

V R Wilson

RINGS OF GUILT

AUSTIN & MACAULEY
PUBLISHERS LTD.

A CIP catalogue record for this title is available from the British
Library.

ISBN 978 1 84963 178 5

www.austinmacauley.com

First Published (2012)
Austin & Macauley Publishers Ltd.
25 Canada Square
Canary Wharf
London
E14 5LB
Printed & Bound in Great Britain

In memory of my beloved husband, greatly missed.

'Absence is to love what wind is to fire;
It extinguishes the small, it inflames the great.'

Histoire Amouruese des Gaules

To family, friends, and people met along life's way who have ensured that the journey has not been dull.

CUBA

Cuba was discovered by Christopher Columbus in 1492. Not until 1508, however, was it realised the place was an island, and one which is as big as all the other Caribbean Islands put together – 780 miles (1250 kilometres) long and 20-120 miles (30-190 kilometres) wide. The climate is tropical and the soil of Cuba's extensive plains is fertile.

From when the island was discovered by Columbus until 1898, except for a brief interlude of British rule 1762-63, Cuba remained under Spanish domination. The defeat of Spain by the United States in 1898 did not lead to independence as expected but instead to American occupation of the island until 1902. In that year an independence treaty was implemented. However, this treaty guaranteed the US continued rights to maintain military bases on the island, hence the naval base at Guantánamo Bay much in the news in recent times.

The establishment of the Republic of Cuba in 1902 did not bring better times for the island's people. The regimes which governed were corrupt, brutal and authoritatian. During 1933-34, there was an abortive attempt to bring change, but the governments which followed ignored the rumblings of unrest. Finally in 1956, Fidel Castro initiated a guerrilla war to oust the then President Fulengio Batista and his supporters and set up a Socialist regime. Three years later, in 1959, the old order was toppled and the Communist state of Cuba was established.

Some maintain that it was American aggression that pushed Fidel Castro into becoming a satellite of the Soviets. He needed economic help and a sugar for oil was struck with the USSR. In 1961, CIA trained Cuban exiles landed in the Bay of Pigs to instigate rebellion but the enterprise was disastrous. Then in 1962 the world was brought to the brink of war by the Cuban missile crisis. Khrushchev backed down. The missiles were removed from Cuba and would not be replaced. In return President Kennedy withdrew nuclear missiles from Turkey. However, the imposition of the trade embargo J F Kennedy imposed remains in force to this day.

The one party state set up by Fidel Castro has improved public health, education and housing considerably but the record on human rights is poor. The end of Soviet subsidies in 1990 and subsequent falling sugar prices led to economic catastrophe which led the Cuban Governments to launch some reforms. The failing health of Fidel Castro in 2008, led to his brother Raúl becoming President of the Council of State and Council of Ministers and he has removed many restrictions, such as on consumer spending for those with foreign currency. Following the events of the recent Arab Spring Raúl Castro seems to have announced that subsequent

Presidents, following the demise of the Castros, will serve only two terms in office.

MAP OF CUBA

CHAPTER 1

The very pale blue sky was cloudless. For late April, however, the air was still very chilly. It had been a long, cold, snowy winter and spring, though dry, had been little warmer.

As he kindly helped Jenny load her suitcase into the boot of her car, Bill, her neighbour, made no secret that he envied her forthcoming holiday. Two weeks of sunshine, in some exotic destination, would be his idea of heaven. Beth, Bill's wife, frowned at such extravagance. If someone else offered to pay, on the other hand, she would be the first to grab the brochures, as Bill himself often stated. Still, they were great neighbours and had been her rock in the year since her beloved husband, Peter, had died.

The previous evening, when packing, she had shared none of Bill's enthusiasm. Quite the contrary, she had questioned her decision for all sorts of reasons. All too late, she was committed. Also Peter had believed in doing things, and going places, while one could.

Once in the car and on her way to Manchester Airport, her negativity left her. For a Sunday morning, the traffic was heavier than expected. So her thoughts were on the road, seeking to be alert for the unexpected. There was no rush, her flight was not until the next day.

Although the route was familiar, she used the sat nav. Its interjections were company, the CDs played the easy listening music she loved, when driving. In consequence, the hundred mile journey had passed pleasantly enough. Only twice had she had cause to be critical of other drivers.

The emptiness of the hotel's front car park surprised her. Inside, too, it seemed unusually quiet. No one appeared to be waiting for the courtesy bus to the airport terminals. Hearing a tall gentleman with a deep voice trying to book a flight to Amsterdam reminded her of the reason.

On April 14, the eruption of a volcano in Iceland had caused chaos. Its ash cloud had caused airports in the UK, as well as many in Europe, to stop all flights for a period of six days. In fact, the large drifting volcanic cloud of ash, as well as any further eruptions, could continue to cause problems for fliers. She hoped not. Her fingers were tightly crossed, her holiday would in no way be affected.

She registered in, then went and moved her car to the long term car park and was pleased to get a good spot. On returning, the key card to the room was available. This pleased her. Strictly speaking, there was still an hour to go to the official start of checking in time for that day.

As Jenny guessed, her room was at the end of the long third floor corridor. She regarded the walk good exercise but might not have done so if she had been pulling along her suitcase. In comparison to the size of cases of many other travellers, hers was small, but it always managed to be heavy. Once an airport sticker 'Beware Heavy' had been stuck on it, and, having escaped such judgement on his case, Peter had loved to tease her before each trip together.

Returning downstairs for a sandwich lunch, she found four people in the bar area. Two gentlemen, sitting separately, were eating while a young couple at a table near the window were engrossed in their books. Only the music which, for once, was not the booming sort, broke the silence.

Having ordered, she chose a table by a pillar. Though her newspaper was tabloid, leafing through its pages seemed to cause loud rustling and to resonate in the pleasant, relaxing atmosphere which encouraged her to linger longer after eating.

Jenny, nevertheless, kept to her resolution to go swimming. The pool, Jacuzzi and sauna were empty. Normally, she would have been delighted to have the place to herself. On this occasion, just having someone to smile at would have been nice. Even on her walk afterwards, there was no one else around but, perhaps, that was because it looked like rain. She only just got back before a heavy downpour.

Late afternoon, reception was busier. Wisely she had booked already for a dinner at seven o'clock. The next two hours spent in her room flew by. Some reading and an indulgent soak in the bath soon swallowed up the time.

Bar meals, early evening, seemed more popular than the restaurant. She chose a table by the window and a seat looking out. With the change to summer time having taken place, it would be interesting to watch outside activity. In any case, as Peter had remarked so often, she could hear the grass grow, so she could eavesdrop on any nearby conversation of interest.

All she could overhear was the argument going on between a couple in their forties. If they were about to start their holiday, it did not bode well. Even the menu seemed to cause disagreement. At least, she enjoyed her meal and her large glass of a very palatable merlot.

Climbing the stairs, rather than taking the lift for which the warring couple were waiting, she concluded it had been a very pleasant day. More would follow, she hoped, during the next fortnight.

Her intuition, not often wrong, gave her the feeling that her forthcoming vacation would be especially remembered. Just why, she could not guess.

CHAPTER 2

Next morning, it was an early start. The time of Jenny's flight to Paris was 09.40. There she would board a flight to Havana. Although she and Peter had travelled extensively, they had never been to any of the Caribbean Islands, nor any part of South America. Her hope was that her next destination would be somewhere on that continent.

The necessary checks and procedures took quite some time. Thus, after a stop for coffee and a bacon roll, some browsing at the shops, in no time it seemed, there was a call to board.

Jenny was pleased to have an aisle seat in row 19, following a requested change to accommodate a family with two young children. The youngest of whom was most unhappy. The four-year-old, named Amanda, declared she was much more grown up as she settled in her seat beside Jenny. Furthermore, having looked hard at Jenny, she told her father that the two of them were going to have a 'conversation'. Her word and not Jenny's, and the serious topic was going to be her eight small Disney character dolls, and her forthcoming trip to Disney World in Paris.

With appropriate comments and observations from Jenny here and there, when prompted, the little girl happily whiled away the time. Thus, for all concerned, it seemed as if they were in Paris 'in a blink of an eye', to quote the child, Amanda, whose vocabulary of words and phrases were very good for her age. It was all quite natural, her innocent charm tempered any precocious forwardness.

In checking in at Manchester, Jenny had been given her boarding card for the onward flight to Havana. Her worry that getting to C91 would present problems was unfounded. The signage at Charles de Gaulle Airport made the task relatively easy.

Reaching the point from where to catch a bus for Terminal C, she got talking to two ladies in their sixties who were going to Cuba for four days on business. What was so pressing to need their presence on the island for such a short time had to remain a mystery, so too, the name of the organisation for which they worked. Conversation was interrupted when an already crowded bus arrived making further chat impossible. If pushed to guess, a religious charity would have been the answer.

Finally, reaching the long concourse at the end of which Gate C91 was situated, the flight screen noted that there would be a fifty minute delay in departure. Even so, the two ladies hastened onwards while foremost in Jenny's mind was finding an outlet from which to buy a bottle of water.

Looking around, she glimpsed a jacket slip from the

top of a bag unnoticed by the owner and her companion. She hurriedly picked it up, but catching up with the couple was not made easy. Her headway was hindered by a large group of young people who were milling around and fooling playfully as they progressed along the concourse.

Eventually she caught up and returned the jacket to its very grateful owner whom she found to be an effusive lady with an American accent. It was when the woman's companion helped 'Rita' put on the jacket to prevent a reoccurrence of its near loss that Jenny noticed his rings. Both identical and distinctive: beautiful blue sapphires, antique gold settings, worn on the third finger of each hand. She had seen them before.

There was an interchange of smiles, but nothing said. The recognition had not been mutual, which was good. She hurried to buy the water, now a real necessity as her throat had gone dry. Indeed, she felt quite shaken.

CHAPTER 3

While pondering over the coincidence, the call to board was made. Passing through the business section to find seat 35H, she glimpsed Rita and Rik. Passing years, fifteen, in fact, had not dimmed her recognition of such unusual jewellery, nor their owner.

The man with Rita was definitely Rik van Huyten. Just as handsome, which was why women fell for him. No doubt, as self-centred as ever for 'leopards did not change their spots'. Clever, devious were other words she could add.

If heading for the same destination, they might meet again. Would she say anything? Might discretion be better to save herself anguish and possible danger? Such were her thoughts as she found her aisle seat. In the same central block of Row 35, on the 777, were three young people, part of a Croatian group. All three seemed only concerned in settling to sleep, in which they succeeded well despite the turbulence encountered.

Right at the start of the flight, the captain had announced that very strong headwinds would add at least an hour to the flight time. In addition, it would be 'a bumpy ride' due to storms which could not be avoided. Not the kind of news any passenger wants to hear, especially not the very nervous ones.

The gentleman across the aisle certainly did not like the turbulence and consoled himself by singing during such periods. His ability to keep in tune failed him when it got particularly bumpy. Hopefully, the previous legs of his journey had been smooth – he had travelled from Pretoria to Johannesburg from where he had flown to Paris.

His accent was strongly South African, his looks Mediterranean. Travelling alone and needing wheelchair assistance at airports, it was presumed by Jenny that his trip to Cuba was prompted by some family connection. However, none of the songs he sang were in Spanish. Whatever his linguistic ability, she had not liked his brusque manner when he spoke to cabin crew.

Touchdown was welcomed by all. The plane was now two and a half hours late which greatly added to the urgency shown by some to depart. The impatient got more impatient, and the downright rude more pushy and aggressive. The very slow, meticulous checking of people and passports did not help the mood of many who were further riled by a second check point. A few expletives in a variety of languages were uttered loudly in frustration.

By the time Jenny got to the relevant luggage carousel the last few cases were being taken off the belt. Nearby, those not already collected, stood waiting to be claimed. Carefully scanning the collection, she could not see her suitcase anywhere. It was then she heard a voice.

"Honey, is your baggage missing as well? Look, we have only got one of our bags."

There was Rita sounding quite tetchy. Rik was approaching with one of the airport baggage attendants.

Immediately, in fluent Spanish, Rita explained the situation. The approach of another passenger made the count three cases, all of which, it was explained, had clear identifying name straps around them. Confident, therefore, that they could not have been mistakenly taken, the attendant was in no doubt that they were only temporarily mislaid.

The optimism began to flag when initial searches by everyone brought no success. Extending the search area brought the 'Eureka' moment to the relief of all concerned. All three cases were found behind a pillar. No one thought of querying their hidden position.

What Jenny was glad about was that others had been in the same predicament and Rita's fluent Spanish had been invaluable. With this hic-cup resolved, she hoped that finding the tour company's airport office, where she was to report to get a taxi, would present no further difficulties. She was tired. It had been a long day. Why, she wondered, did people put themselves through such trauma for a holiday?

Before departing on their separate ways, Rita had called out that she would phone. Earlier she had inquired where Jenny was staying and had given their hotel name in exchange. The inquiry had stemmed from her expressed concern about Jenny being on her own and with only a smattering of Spanish, and seemed very genuine.

If they did meet again, would she remind Rik of their earlier meeting? He had given no indication of recognising her, but then he had no real reason to do so. After all, they had met but briefly and his interest in people had no attachment or depth. Such were her thoughts as her taxi lurched. Cyclists had no lights and the street lighting was poor.

The roads were very wet. There had been a storm and it would have been easy to aquaplane if any vehicle had been speeding. Besides asking from where she came and comments like, 'Big storm earlier," the driver was not the chatty sort. Even Jenny's attempts in Spanish received only monosyllabic answers. The twelve mile journey from the airport seemed long as a result.

Fortunately, formalities at reception, on arrival, were minimal and there was a buggy waiting to take her to her accommodation. The hotel was village style, situated between two of the three berthing canals of the marina with the sea beyond. A very distinctive location, as she was to appreciate during her stay.

The porter was keen to show the boats of the marina right below the balcony of her room which was on the first floor. The bedroom block, built on concrete stilts, consisted of two floors of eight rooms, and was the one which offered the best views in the complex.

Already nearing the next day, even in Cuban time, which was five hours behind British Summer time, Jenny was more than eager for sleep having been up almost twenty-four hours. Still, she quickly unpacked and showered before collapsing on her bed. It had been quite a day.

CHAPTER 4

Jenny woke early and was amongst the first to breakfast when the restaurant opened at 7 a.m. The other early risers were part of a group of some thirty Venezuelans. Not all breakfasted before being picked up by coach at 7.30 a.m. to return at around 5 p.m. The smartness of their dress, and the bags they carried, led her to guess that this all male group was attending some course of study.

Those, who breakfasted, intended to set themselves up well for the day ahead, whatever that might be. The breakfast buffet offered a wide choice and the Chef of the Day was kept busy cooking omelettes. She always envied the ease with which professional cooks cracked eggs.

The whole environment added to her enjoyment of her early morning repast. The view was good, the sky was blue, it was pleasantly warm, what more could one want? Thus, revived and in good spirits, Jenny was ready for a leisurely day interspersed with some swimming.

In fact, the draw of the pool was so strong that, less than half an hour later, she was taking her first dip. Once over the initial chill, the water caressed the body. Unhindered by anyone else, she amused herself happily swimming all ways across the pool's quite reasonable expanse. Some guests heading for the restaurant smiled in her direction. From the numbers she observed, it rather indicated that the hotel was not overly busy.

An hour later the loungers were beginning to attract the sun worshippers, but no one else ventured into the water, which was why she lingered. Still, she was aware she needed to change money and get her bearings by exploring a little of the area round about.

In Cuba, tourists use 'pesos convertible', while Cubans use 'pesos cubanos'. This is the currency in which they are paid and buy their staple commodities. The people have ration books which ensures they have basic food and do not starve. To buy more, other than fruit and vegetables, or to buy 'luxury' goods, they need 'pesos convertible' which are expensive for them to buy. Each tourist peso they buy costs them twenty-four of their own 'pesos cubanos'.

This is what makes the island's tourist industry so attractive to work in. The tips make the recipients prosperous. In consequence, able and intelligent young people choose to work in hotels, bars and restaurants, rather than undertake lengthy studies at university to end up in the professions earning less. Cuba might be in need of hard currency but, in embracing tourism, it needs to be alert to the social consequences.

All this Jenny had read about before coming and it was all confirmed the more she spoke to people about life on the island. The small nearby supermarket stocked just the bare necessities with no choice of brands as back home. Here she saw a Ration Book being used for flour, rice and sugar.

It was really just curiosity that had made her look in at the shop. As yet she was without money to buy anything. At reception, she had been directed to the Hotel 'El Viejo y El Mer', a fifteen minute walk away to change her pounds sterling. Why the transaction could not be carried out that morning at her own hotel, her Spanish was not good enough to understand. Some night have been annoyed about this but she was unconcerned.

The marina and the hotel at which she was staying, had been built as a result of a deep sea fishing competition which Ernest Hemmingway sponsored and which Fidel Castro patronised. The American author and Nobel Prize winner lived in Cuba for many years. Her destination recalled, in Spanish, the title of one of his books.

Strangely, of the two books by Hemingway she had read, namely *For Whom the Bell Tolls* and *The Old Man and the Sea* (El Viejo y el Mer), the latter was the one she best remembered. So, as she walked along, she challenged herself to recall and summarise the story.

The old man, Santiago, after a long spell without a catch, finally hooked the largest marlin he had ever seen. Having attached it to the side of his boat, he dreamt of the fortune it would bring him and the legend he would become. Sadly, however, when he gets back to harbour, all that remains is the backbone and tail, the sharks have devoured the flesh. Santiago has no choice but to continue to dream, as his humble existence continues.

Supposedly Santiago was based on the Captain and Cook aboard Hemingway's boat *The Pilar*. Her thoughts were interrupted as she arrived at her destination, which seemed to be a rehabilitation centre for young and old with orthopaedic problems. Outside, the building, a concrete structure, seemed to shout that it, too, was not well and needed rehabilitation.

Inside, the foyer area indicated some improvement, but a prescription for brighter colours, a more vibrant décor, was judged to be needed. At least, the charming young woman at the Bureau de Change, even in the gloom of her small cubicle, quietly oozed a personality to enthral. Just meeting her was worth the walk and her English was good.

Then as she was leaving, she heard a commanding voice say, "Inglesa."

Turning, she saw a very Spanish looking woman in a wheelchair, who might once had been a flamenco beauty. Jenny concluded that she was the dowager who held court in this establishment.

"Nice to see a smart, brightly dressed young woman in this place," she added, before being wheeled away.

"Muchas gracias for the word 'young'," Jenny shouted into the shadowy gloom.

Jenny did like clothes and always managed to look smart and stylish without spending a fortune. In hot climes, she aimed to appear cool by avoiding over exposure to the sun. Her comfortable, pale lilac, patterned beach dress of combed cotton was loose enough to let air at her body. Her white hat trimmed with navy ribbon kept her face and head protected.

Therefore, although it was getting hot, she decided she would venture further to explore. The nearby sea wall needed repair. The pounding waves had demolished a small section completely. Looking back towards the marina, it was clear that landscaping the land between its berthing canal and the sea would enhance the area. Certainly it should not be built on, but become a smart, planted promenade. This, however, was Cuba, a hard pressed Communist island 'where everything always creaked, or spluttered'. On that comment, she would reserve judgement.

CHAPTER 5

Back at the hotel, enjoying a long, cool drink after her walk and exploration, she was delighted to meet a couple from the UK. Ted and Barbara Miller, who hailed from Lancashire but lived near Barnsley in Yorkshire, were equally glad to meet her and to talk. Along with three other people, they were 'victims' of the volcanic ash and airport shut downs. As a result, their Cuban holiday had been extended by over two weeks. Only that morning they had been told they would leave for Manchester on Friday, April 30, along with Jane Eaton whom they described as a lovely, widowed lady.

They added that, without their presence, this unavoidable lengthy delay, would have made her quite distraught. This indeed Jane Eaton confirmed when she met up with Jenny later. The other two British people were leaving earlier, namely the following day, but were having to fly to Panama City from where they would fly to London. Whilst hearing all this, she was praying, quietly, that she would not be faced with any such problems.

An amiable couple, Ted and Barbara were very eager

to pass on information, and advice, they had gathered the hard way. The conversation continued over lunch after which the Miller's declared that their intention was a siesta, reading and cards on the balcony.

Jenny wanted to arrange some trips and so went to find Jacinta at her desk in the foyer of the main building. This short, slight, pale skinned young woman, her attractive face framed by short, shining, dark brown hair, had been highly praised by the Millers; praise that Jenny thought she more than duly deserved. Her English was good, she was informative and exceedingly helpful. The two were to have many conversations.

Not wishing to look too far ahead, Jenny booked for 'Old Havana' the following day, Wednesday, and then Vinales on the Friday. She wanted to see around, but in a balanced, relaxed way to properly digest the environment. Books said that Cuba was 'inseparable from its politics and Communism'. The island's people, it was said, were resilient, forebearing, happy despite shortages with the 'music in their souls' hard to deny.

On leaving Jacinta, she spent the time swimming, reading and looking at some of the cruisers and yachts. The ocean going craft she looked down on from her balcony was registered in Norway. On board were two good looking men unmistakably in love with their boat and each other and seemingly oblivious to all else!

Later after an enjoyable dinner, she joined Jane, Ted and Barbara at the Pool Bar for coffee. The Millers did not linger long. Jane commented that they never did and it was something she regretted.

Widowed three years, she had found the first two years exceedingly difficult, she had gone to pieces. Only during this last year had her confidence gradually returned, along with success for her one woman outside catering business. Consequently, her extended stay in Cuba was a worry. She did not want it to set back her work.

Then, having brought them two 'night caps', she suddenly excused herself having seen Hans settle at a distant table. He had been mentioned by the Millers; how they had befriended him and were trying to improve his very limited English.

Before Jenny had time to think, a gentleman all in white sat at the table.

"Pardone, a beautiful lady should not sit and drink alone, I keep company," he uttered with a smile and nod.

'Ooops!' She thought in panic. 'Jane where are you?'

"The lady will be back," she said sharply.

"Then I go," he replied. "My son and his wife," he indicated to a nearby table, where a couple seated nodded their acknowledgement. They were a smart, good looking twosome, not long married was her guess. The father, as said, was dressed all in white: shirt, trousers, shoes, watch strap and large white fedora.

'Not polite to sit at a lady's table with your hat on,' she thought, and, in other circumstances, would have stated so out loud.

Tables around were now suddenly occupied but, why be driven away, she told herself. She would finish her drink and then go. After all, the man was just being gallant. He reminded her of Zorba. There was a look of Anthony Quinn about his rugged, swarthy complexioned face, probably mid-sixties in age. Moreover, he knew well that his penetrating gaze was unnerving her.

Sensing this, he introduced himself and offered other information so that she would relax, enjoy her drink and the beautiful evening. His English was clipped, strongly accented and, as he added, very limited.

"Vidal Rivero, son Rodrigo, daughter-in-law Maria, from Panama. Me. Mexican. Business Acapulco and Cancun. Wife Elena, dead fourteen months."

Pointing at her wedding ring, he believed Jenny would understand the sadness.

She did, and the loneliness, she certainly did. As yet though, she was not ready to move on to any flirtation if that was Vidal's intention. Finishing her drink, she got up to leave, declining the offer of an escort. Jane's grin in calling out 'good night', indicating her amusement at Vidal's interest, was not appreciated!

On opening the door of her room, she found a note. It read:

> Phone call from Rita Carballo.
> Hope you OK. Keep Saturday evening, May 1, free for dinner. 6.30 p.m. Taxi will collect.

The day had passed without a thought about Rita and

Rik. Despite the surname given by Rita, her belief that it was Rik van Huyten never wavered. The invitation would be accepted.

CHAPTER 6

The pick up time for the tour of 'Old Havana' was 8.30 a.m. but as she ambled to the foyer at 8.10 a.m., she was greeted by a young woman who was to be the guide. Lena had arrived by taxi to join Jenny at the first pick up point for the coach. This was to join be a bonus as it gave her a good thirty minutes to talk to Lena about life in Cuba.

Aged 34, Lena was a qualified lawyer, married to a cardio-vascular surgeon, aged 38. In a good season, she could exceed, in tips, her husband's annual salary. This was why she had paid for herself to attend language school to become fluent in English and French.

Since 2008, when Raúl Castro was elected president of the Council of State and Council of Ministers, the restriction on consumer spending, for those with foreign currency and 'pesos convertible' had been lifted. This had meant that Cubans could own mobile phones, DVD players, have more computer and internet access, as well as stay at tourist hotels on the beach. The following, and, subsequent weekend, the hotel at the marina was witness to how those with disposable currency were using the privilege, and taking advantage of the weekend package deals on offer.

The arrival of the coach allowed Lena to ignore the cheeky inquiry as to whether Fidel Castro was still alive. Later, she did tell the group that although he had not been seen in public for some time, he was believed to follow still the custom of moving residence every few days. This routine was established to avoid assassination attempts by the CIA, rumoured with having tried and failed some sixty-nine times.

Lena, on being given confirmation of the number of pick up points, the number and nationality of her passengers, was not a happy bunny. The total was forty-two: thirty-nine Argentinians, two Danes and Jenny. What concerned her was that the Argentinians lacked a sense of time and did not abide by any time constraints set.

Jenny felt a sympathy that was to increase during the tour which also confirmed her initial worry that the size of the group was too big to keep tabs on in a busy city. It also meant that Lena's time for herself and the Danish couple was reduced to a minimum. Picking up a little from Lena's often lengthy spiel, along with glances at her small guidebook, Jenny excused her for curtailing what she said in English at each stop.

Since becoming an UNESCO World Heritage site in 1992, a lot of restoration work had been carried out. This task was neither easy, nor cheap, and, in 2008, suffered quite a setback when a hurricane overturned years of work. In its day, Havana was regarded as the finest colonial city in the Americas.

The tour began at the Fortress El Morro, built in the sixteenth century, which like the larger fortification of La Cabana, was built by Spanish Conquistadores to protect the harbour from attack. The stop was meant as a vantage point from which to view the city's skyline and take photographs, so was to last but fifteen minutes. Spying craft stalls within the ramparts, the Argentinians lost track of time. Consequently, they added another twenty minutes to the stop with no need.

There was no stop at La Cabana from where each evening at 9 p.m., a cannon is fired; a custom from the time it signalled the closure of the doors in the city walls. Actually, this fortress was built after a short period of British rule during the Seven Years War (1756-1763), following which the island was exchanged for Florida.

The walking tour began in the Plaza de San Francisco where tourists are greeted by the women 'cigar vendors' in their traditional and colourful dress. The menfolk were very keen to be photographed with any, or all, of the bevy of beauties. The vibrant colours, and the playing of four musicians, began to open up for Jenny, the magic of Havana.

Almost all followed the custom of touching the pointed finger of the statue of 'El Cabellero de Paris' for luck when passing it on the way to Plaza Vieja. On reaching the square, where the frontages of the buildings, restored and newly painted in pastel colours, gleamed in the sun, the group had begun to straggle. It was clear the interest of some, in the history, had waned already, while others hung on every word and dominated Lena's time and attention with their questions.

Under supervision, a group of young school children were using the square to play competitive, relay games quite oblivious to the history and restoration work. If walls could talk, she thought, what tales they could tell, and, as the group wandered through the narrow streets, she imagined that, in the early hours, there might be a ghostly whisper, or two. Her wandering imagination was halted by Lena's sudden panic that some of the group had disappeared. The prodigals did return but progress had been delayed again.

With the Argentinians duly corralled, Lena spent some time talking to them near the Hotel Ambos Mundos. On this occasion, Jenny was unconcerned about its length. The reason was that she was happy to listen to the pianist at the Ambos Mundos Bar, playing beautifully classic, popular tunes. Someone would have been playing in the same style in Hemingway's time there.

The renown of Hotel Ambos Mundos stems from the fact that the author wrote much of *For Whom The Bell Tolls* while he occupied Room 511, on and off, for a couple of years in the late 1930s. The book is based on the Spanish Civil War which he covered as a journalist.

Thinking of Spain made Jenny recall how proudly the Bull Ring in Ronda featured photographs of Hemingway, a great patron of bull fighting. To her, it was a very barbaric sport and therefore, she would never read Hemingway's book *Death In the Afternoon*.

Time to move on and just as well. The tunes being

played were so nostalgic that tears were welling up. There were four Argentinians to whom she would not want to show any kind of weakness. Every time they came alongside, they uttered 'Las Malvinas'. She sympathised if they had lost someone in the Falklands conflict, but their behaviour was inexcusable.

Whilst by the Palacio de las Capitanes Generales, on the western side of Plaza des Armas, a small procession of colourfully dressed entertainers on stilts passed by with the cigar vendors now collecting for charity. The vivacity of the group, and their acrobatic skills, seemed to lift the spirits of all around, besides delighting the keen photographers.

The Plaza dates to the city's foundation in 1519 and consists of so much of interest, a fort, a neo classical temple, a luxurious hotel and a museum of the city of Havana housed in the palacio mentioned. There are stalls of second hand books to be found there on most days. Even in passing, it would be hard not to notice that Fidel Castro was a popular subject for authors. Again, Jenny wondered if he was alive, or in an embalmed state waiting for the right moment to announce that he had died?

A 'mojito and tapas' stop after the Cathedral square was mentioned much to everyone's delight. The square was crowded, there was filming taking place: a balcony scene was being rehearsed. Not for *Romeo and Juliet*, however, but for some political oratory to which, on cue, the crowd below were being tutored to re-act.

Jenny used the opportunity, while Lena was in full

Spanish flow, to enter the cathedral. According to a Cuban writer, the building was 'music set in stone'. The baroque façade is glorious, but it was the cathedral's not too ornate interior that, in Jenny's opinion, gave the place dignity.

The twenty minute stop for some great live music by three talented, elderly musicians whilst sipping a 'mojito' and partaking of tapas, was a very pleasant interlude.

The bar man's skill was applauded as he lined the glasses and with a fine tuned eye, prepared the much awaited drink: rum, soda water, lime juice, sugar, ice and fresh mint. Had there been time, most, who indulged, would have ordered another, and maybe another, forgetting their intoxicating punch.

Here Lena exerted her authority and thwarted any attempt to linger by herding everyone out and down a short narrow alleyway to where the coach was waiting. The tour was meant to give everyone a comprehensive glimpse of what the city had to offer and was not going to be curtailed through running late.

At the next stop, about half the party climbed the steep steps to enter, at a cost, the monumental Capitolio building – a replica of the Capitol Building in Washington DC. The large bronze door which, in pictures, chart the island's history, and the immense main gallery were worth the climb to see. All distances in Cuba are measured from a central spot in the floor beneath the Dome.

Outside, there are always vintage American cars from the 1950s to be seen which creates an attraction always for tourists. About to take some photographs, she heard her name called. In the back of a Cadillac, dating from 1956, which pulled up beside her, were Rita and Rik. The car, and its driver, along with an official guide, had been hired for a day tour of Havana.

How ideal, Jenny enviously thought.

Rita was eager to be assured her invitation for Saturday, May 1, had been received and clearly pleased it was being accepted. The taxis were their responsibility as was the evening. It was Rik who added it would be a small intimate group and that he was sure she would enjoy the evening and be quite at ease in the company.

There was much to intrigue her. Who would be there? Was there a special reason for the dinner party? Had Rik begun to wonder if they had met before? Rita was not his usual type, unless he had changed. She was no pushover; charming, effusive, smart, attractive were words which could be used to describe Rita from a brief acquaintance.

Jenny wondered if, as with Rik, it might be a veneer and beneath was a person with steely determination that no one would stand in the way of her goals. How bitchy, she reprimanded herself as she decided, like the two Danes to view Plaza de la Revolution from the coach. Not so the Argentinians, many of whom walked round most of the square's perimeter, around a mile. Yet the mural, an iron sculpture of Che Guevara, was better viewed from afar.

The last stop at a Rum Factory also took much longer than was necessary, after which there was the slow process of getting everyone back to their hotels. It was almost 6 p.m. before a weary and hungry Jenny was back at the marina. Nevertheless the lure of the pool attracted her into having a quiet swim before darkness fell.

Later, dining alone in the small 'a la carte' Portofino Restaurant, she could not help feeling sad at not having anyone to talk to and recall the day.

CHAPTER 7

Jenny greatly enjoyed her early morning swim and having the pool to herself. Afterwards she walked as far as the Post Office to buy postcards and was accompanied on the way back by Jacinta. Queues for busses in Cuba are always long and the many stops make journeys slow. Sometimes staff are lucky to get lifts from coaches heading to their hotel, being recognised by their uniforms. No such luck for Jacinta that morning.

On reaching the hotel foyer, their conversation was abruptly finished by a foursome eager to book tours. Deciding to have coffee at the lobby bar, she drifted into conversation with a young Chinese woman whom she had seen around, and with whom she had exchanged smiles.

Lee (Sun Lui) needed no prompting to tell her that she was on a year's academic study in Canada. Her Canadian companion was enjoying a holiday romance, but she had a husband back in Shanghai. He was involved in the export trade which her sojourn in the west would help. Just how was a point she did not develop.

Although proud of her academic achievements, her

parents who were described as 'old school' Chinese, hated her westernisation, her 'corruption'. This led to quite a deep discussion between the two on politics, economics and differing philosophies. Delighted that Jenny had been to China and had visited her home town of Chungking even, Lee clearly felt she could relax and voice her views and criticisms freely. Yet, China was her home and she would return there.

While walking to the restaurant for lunch, some heavy drops of rain were felt. At that time, the clouds, which had appeared, did not indicate that darker, heavier ones were soon to follow bringing torrential rain for most of the day, thereafter. She had her fingers crossed, the next day would be hot and sunny again as she had booked to go to Vinales.

Poor Hans, she thought, was he getting this rain?

Briefly the previous evening, the German had told her he was going to Vinales when he approached her to inquire about the Millers' and Jane Eaton whom he had not seen. Neither had she, and still had not glimpsed them. With their extended holiday about to end, she trusted all was well.

After lunch, she decided her room was the best option. Time would not hang heavy. There were cards to write, her holiday journal to update, that neglected book to finish and there was always the TV to view. Actually, she had not switched it on before and now did so to catch a snippet of financial news on CNN. What she heard was depressing and she quickly turned the TV off. Peter had believed holiday time should be free from concerns, therefore, no newspapers or TV – she would adhere to that.

Looking out, the gloom of the scene could not be ignored. Still, everywhere looks sad in the rain. The yachts looked unhappy at their drenching. The two guards, who had been sitting playing cards in the sentry box, had slumped into sleep. Nothing stirred once the wind had dropped.

Coming to six o' clock, suitably dressed in a plastic rain coat and armed with a bright umbrella, carried for such emergencies, she braved her way to the lobby bar. Avoiding all puddles was impossible but, at least, no vehicle passed to splatter her.

Never having tried a Rum Punch, she decided to order one. The under manager and public relations officer were eager to engage her in conversation. Not able to travel from Cuba, they were keen to know about hotels and tourism elsewhere. Staff, it seemed, had concluded that Jenny was a smart, dignified, intelligent, well-travelled lady. Embarrassed by such a list of complementary attributes, she was equally gratified by it.

Despite the continuing rain, she felt elated, but refrained from 'singing in the rain', as she made her way to the small Portofino Restaurant for dinner. The ambience suited her though she missed the music of the quintet which played each evening in the Kilimanjaro Restaurant above. For coffee afterwards, the rain having eased greatly, she made her way to the pool bar where several of the Venezuelans were playing cards. The cards, and the game, she had never come across before.

Seeing her interest, and that of Lee who was already standing at the bar, one of the group came over to try and explain the rules to both of them.

Both concluded that the main element consisted of bluff but was different from, and more fun than, Poker. They were invited to sit and play, but both declined especially as the band had come over from the restaurant earlier than usual. The singer encouraged Jenny and Lee, who were moving to the music, to follow him in a conga style dance, which some of the non-card players amongst the Venezuelans joined.

The music changed and she was about to make her way to a table when she was virtually grabbed by Vidal, who expertly steered her into the steps of a slow tango, at which, it was clear, he was an expert.

"Relax, enjoy, have fun," he whispered.

Like Vidal, others had appeared and many were dancing. A glance at Lee, also with a partner and dancing, showed her delight with the impromptu 'dancing session'. Giggling, she winked at Jenny.

Whilst the music played, all the dancers remained on the floor, only when it stopped did people move back to their tables. Unnerved by the music, Vidal's closeness and her memories, Jenny wanted to hurry away, but the barman indicated he had an Americano coffee for her. Considering it very churlish to refuse, especially as it was what she had come for except the dancing intervened, she nodded her acceptance.

Vidal jumped to carry it to a table and then joined her when he had got himself a drink. Sitting he thanked her for dancing with him.

"We dance again and you become good."

Thank you for that vote of confidence, she thought as she tried to explain, without success, that she was not ready to dance with a partner. Too many memories of how she and Peter had enjoyed dancing together, especially in the still of an evening, near a foreign shore.

"Your heart must stop crying, like mine has now done," he whispered to her, making her eyes fill up.

Coffee finished, he escorted her to the stairwell leading up to her room. They had walked in silence, the rain had stopped, the stars twinkled, only the puddles remained, a reminder of how wet it had been. In saying 'goodnight' he kissed her hand, and, in walking away, he shouted back, "Hasta luego!"

His strong musk scented aftershave seemed to cling in the air as she climbed the stairs. There would be much to remember from her Cuban holiday.

CHAPTER 8

Early morning, a taxi came to collect Jenny to take her to the Commodore Hotel where the coach would pick her up for her trip to Vinales. Within five minutes of arrival, the coach duly arrived and being the last passenger to be collected, there was no delay in getting on to the main highway (autopista). Julia, the guide, was a tall, well rounded black woman with a strong American accent even though she had never left the island.

Immediately, she made the very international mix of thirty people aware of her rule to ensure all had a lovely day, namely to be on time always. Indeed, the bonnie Julia proved to be an excellent leader of the pack, humorous, informative, without overloading her listeners.

The highway was straight with little traffic, so the coach was soon at its first stop, a small neat village of one storey dwellings, with a cigar packing factory at its centre. The word 'factory' might bring to mind a large building, which was not so in this case. The one storey building was only double the size of the residences around, with only twenty workers in total: the atmosphere was more of a cottage industry.

Everyone knows that Cuban cigars are reputed to be the world's finest, but Jenny was not alone in being amazed at the vast range of sizes, all named. There was no denying the dexterity of the men and women who rolled the cigars, while the packers needed a keen eye to ensure all cigars in a box matched exactly for colour and size. Throughout, quality control was strict, and not unexpectedly, the building exuded a rich, distinctive aroma.

Trade at the shop was brisk, from boxes to a single cigar, that necessary souvenir of Cuba. Then it was on to a small tobacco farm to see the plants and the leaves drying in steep roofed barns. The small functional cottage of the owners was shown with pride. It made Jenny feel somewhat guilty at the space she enjoyed at home, in both house and large garden and the possessions and clothes she had. It made her wonder if the really rich, especially those living in poor countries, ever felt uncomfortable about their wealth and bounty in comparison to the poverty seen around them?

Near to the farm was a shop and café and having been told lunch would be late afternoon, all heeded the advice to have a drink and snack. Looking for a table, she heard her name and four people indicating for her to join them. They must have noted it, she assumed, when Julia collected her at the Commodore.

The four were Canadians from Vancouver, who were staying at the Hotel National de Cuba, where they had become acquainted with Rita and Rik. They, too, had been invited to Saturday's soiree and had been told a

Jenny Moran would be joining the party. From what a member of the hotel staff let slip, the number would be ten so they wondered if Jenny knew who the other three would be. They wanted to know as well how she knew the couple and whether she was a long-time friend.

That she was unable to tell them anything about the couple, nor if there was a special reason for Saturday's dinner party was a disappointment. There was much about the two that was intriguing all of them, plus there was the mystery regarding the other guests with which to toy. No one else from the hotel, on that the Canadians were positive.

Who then? That question was in all their minds as they boarded the coach again with everyone dutifully on time. The route now left the level, palm dotted plains, to wind through beautiful lush countryside towards the Guaniguarico Mountains and the hidden Vinales valley.

A stop at a viewing point above the valley revealed its picturesque beauty. Amongst the deeply green patchwork of fields below were 'mogotes'. These are sheer sided limestone formations, rising high from the ground, which are covered in thick vegetation. Jenny remembered how in Guilin, in China, similar limestone outcrops are called 'karsts', and there, they have inspired thousands of paintings. Nobody said anything about Cuban poets and painters being roused likewise by the beauty. Perhaps that was because in Vinales, the landscape was gentler and less moody.

Tethered nearby, and much photographed, was a saddled bull, a Brahmin type breed, quite unconcerned about the activity around. Oxen are still used to plough, small tractors being a rarity and some 'guajiros' ride their bulls, hence the saddle. Mostly though, the 'guajiros', cowboy farmers, go round their small holdings on horseback. Agriculture is still not mechanised and the diminishing rural population means that school children are used to help harvest crops – a compulsory part of the education of all.

The coach halted next to allow all to see the 'Mural of Pre-History' painted on the side of a limestone 'mogote' – a curiosity rather than a treasure. About to leave from the car park were the Carballos whom Jenny spotted first. She called to the Canadians and they all approached the car, which this time was not a vintage Cadillac, but the guide was the same person as on their tour of Havana. Greetings were cordial but, stating that they were trying to cram a lot into the day, they excused the briefness of the chat. Wishing all a very pleasant day, they sped on their way.

A shrug of the shoulders by one of the Canadians, along with the facial expressions of the others, seemed to reflect Jenny's mental query: what to make of that? Not that it was important, enjoying the trip was the main priority especially as the weather was glorious again. However, she did hear Julia say that Vinales had experienced no rain the previous day.

In passing further limestone cliffs, attention was drawn to the lattice work created naturally by stalactites and stalagmites. Soon after, they were off the coach again to visit the Indian Cave Complex (Cueva del Indio) whereby they would enter on one side of a hill and emerge on the other. A lengthy, narrow winding path, around and between rocks, and pillars, led to an underground river which, in small groups, they explored further aboard a boat. It was not mentioned, yet she had read that, in the past, one of the boats had been stolen by Cubans seeking to sail to Florida. The venture failed. So, while looking around at the features pointed out to them, she wondered if she would be brave enough to consider crossing sixty miles of sea in a small open boat? Pushed by desperation, then maybe.

Pangs of hunger must have been felt by all because, on emerging from the caves, no one dallied on the way to the nearby restaurant. The four resident musicians were playing as people took their places at the set table in order of arrival. Thus, Jenny and the Canadians were separated which had disappointed them, especially as those around them offered no conversation while they noticed much laughter and chat at Jenny's end of the table.

The food was tasty with everything cleared in all three courses. A relaxed, congenial atmosphere had been created by the musicians and their serenading of Jenny and another of the ladies, had added an element of fun to everyone's enjoyment. The laughter and chat continued as people boarded the coach for the short ride to Vinales town where some were staying overnight. This allowed the rest a strict thirty minutes to wander the arcaded main street.

Many, like Jenny, just sat on the benches around a

paved square where six young children, aged about eight, were dancing the salsa. They were great movers and delighted the new onlookers with their expertise. In turn, the children were thrilled to be applauded and photographed. An elderly gentleman, keen not to be out-danced by the youngsters, joined them to show his skill. He might have had a very lined face, but his agility was remarkable and that 'music in the soul' clear to see.

Fresh air and the heat of the day, for most, led to a late siesta on the way back. Noticing Jenny awake, the young Polish man, sitting across the aisle, began talking to her and them moved over to make conversation easier. He also wished to practice his English which he considered not as good as his German and Russian.

Always interested in people and their views, Jenny welcomed the easy chat which followed on a whole range of topics. Why is there so much discord, she reflected, when as individuals, people's opinions about important subjects are so alike? The return journey, in consequence, flew by. In no time, it seemed, she was being dropped off right outside the pathway which led to her room. Climbing the stairs, she concluded it had been a very worthwhile and enjoyable excursion which had revealed the quiet, unhurried Cuba.

With her table for dinner booked for 8.30 p.m., she had forty-five minutes to get ready so there was no need to rush. When she got to the Portofino, it was busier than usual but then she was dining later. Her table awaited, leaving a small tip each evening, seemed to get her special attention. A table of four men, Canadians, she guessed, were heard to remark about this. Not having seen them before, she guessed, as with their nationality, that they were newly arrived. Her presumption was that they were on the island on business. She had heard something about a tourism conference.

Leaving, she immediately walked into the quintet and behind them Vidal and Rodrigo. Her hope of escape with just a courteous smile of recognition was foiled when the musicians began to play 'For The Lady to Have One Dance'. It was a salsa and fortunately she had received a few lessons in anticipation of her holiday. Her skill came as a surprise to the fedora hatted Vidal, along with the fact that she had not hesitated in accepting the invitation to dance, acknowledging the sense of fun intended by the band.

When the music stopped, for the first time Rodrigo spoke more than a greeting, informing her in good English that there were four Canadians at the hotel for a conference and nine newly arrived Brits on holiday. How Jenny hated that word 'Brits' and hoped that the newcomers were not the sort that term usually meant. Thanking him for the information she added she would wait until the following day before meeting up with them.

Saying 'gracias' for the music and dance and 'buenos noches' to all, she turned in the direction of her room. Before she had covered any distance, Vidal caught up with her and fell into stride beside her. Feeling uneasy, she determined to say nothing unless he began to chat which he did telling her Maria had to leave for Panama as her mother was ill, appendicitis. It surprised her that he knew she had been to Vinales, even if he had seen the coach, there was no indication of the destination to which it had been.

At her stairwell, he took her hand, kissed it, wished her pleasant dreams, then left. His intentions, she concluded, were harmless enough; he was merely a roguish, flirtatious tease whose attentions would soon stop.

A note had been slipped under the door of her room with an apology it has not been delivered earlier. It was a response from the Millers, and Jane, to her note of good wishes. Somewhere high over the mid-Atlantic, they must be dozing happily, finally on their way home.

CHAPTER 9

May 1st, International Labour Day, is always a fiesta when Cubans gather in the stark, large concourse of Revolution Square in Havana. Usually the crowd numbers over a million and later new-casts revealed 2010 to be no exception. In his heyday, Fidel Castro regaled those gathered with lengthy speeches, one of which holds the record for lasting over ten hours. Nevertheless, his verbosity and long windedness never dampened his popularity. In contrast, his brother Raúl, not having the charisma, or oratory, says little or nothing, at the May Day celebrations nowadays.

The day being a holiday, the hotel's thrice daily courtesy bus into Old Havana was not running. So with more guests around the complex, and locals coming in on day passes, the pool area was busy. From early morning, staff at the pool bar were rushed, catering for the demand for snacks from their compatriots determined to enjoy the lack of rationing.

Being an early bird, Jenny managed some swimming before the pool began to fill and youngsters began to play therein. Watching people pass, she guessed that she had seen, at least, four English speakers make their way to the loungers near the bar area. When she made her way for coffee, she found she was right and it was they who spoke first, having been told the English lady would help them to know their way around.

It was not the passing on of useful information, which she had been given by the Millers on her arrival, and adding to it from her own experience, that niggled her. It was the fact that the supposed tour representative for the company, through which they had all travelled, remained conspicuous by her absence. After the weekend, she would seek to resolve the matter.

When the other five British newcomers arrived to join the group, she suggested that they moved to some tables where it would be easier to talk. This gave one couple the opportunity to order further martinis, while the rest chose coffee or beer. All came from the South East and had flown from Gatwick to Madrid to get an onward flight to Havana. It was on landing that they had become acquainted.

The Bensons were of Jamaican origin. Delroy was tall, thin, reserved and thoughtful, while Patsy was tall, rounded and hyperactive. Both were in their forties. The Fowlers were of a similar age, while the Crofts were in their late seventies with poor Harriet having to watch Bob's tendency to suddenly blurt out something of no significance. The Robinson's, the martini drinkers, were both short, overweight, vocal about their travels and his wheeling and dealing which afforded them a comfortable lifestyle. Rough diamonds with a small 'd', one might say.

Lastly there was Helen, a somewhat bitter divorcee in her fifties who proved to be very much a loner. Later it was concluded that she spent too much time in her room with her iPod, quite unnecessarily. The rest of the disparate group, Jenny included, having been thrown together, met up at the pool bar after dinner to chat and joke, making it a really pleasurable part of the holiday.

Helen noticed that Jenny was being watched carefully by a young man, who by the description, she took to be Rodrigo. When a few minutes later, she added that he had been joined by an older man wearing a hat, the teasing began. It would seem the dancing episode, the previous evening, had been noticed by most, even from across the pool. The more Jenny blushed, or tried to explain, the more she was teased.

Vidal and Rodrigo were well aware of the group's interest in them and they acknowledged each glance with a gracious nod of recognition. Jenny told them, they were acting like silly teenagers which led to the following retort, in chorus:

"Oh, Miss, is he your boyfriend?"

From the corner of her eye, she noticed the Riveros leave, but decided to make no remark about it, especially as the group's attention had diverted to some activity in the pool. The respite from the teasing was not to last however. The waiter brought over to the table three bottles of Spanish Cava, while another followed with a tray of ten glasses.

"Compliments of Mr Rivero to Mrs Moran and

friends."

At her request, the waiter did the honours. The popping of corks was greeted with general hilarity and an eagerness to partake. There were compliments on the vintage. Helen's remark that the glasses were wrong, while telling Jenny she should be flattered by the attention, led to some teasing comments like 'party pooper' and she was only jealous. Her lack of humour, or ability to relax and be convivial was obvious.

Initially, Jenny had felt in no way flattered, on the contrary, she had thought, how could he, the mischievous old rogue, knowing she was already being teased.

Hopefully Vidal realised that the teasing stemmed from the fact that their dance, the previous evening, had been seen and not because she had said anything. It was a gesture which would have cost him, so maybe she should be flattered. Her confidence was boosted.

After lunch, she made her way to the small salon for a body and facial massage, followed by a shampoo and blow dry, all in preparation for the evening ahead in the company of the Carballos. Indulging herself in this way was always part of her routine on holiday. Some massages, particularly in parts of Asia, had been quite stimulating, if not rough, but not so here. The experience was most relaxing and pleasurable, carried out by a lovely Cuban lady, aged about forty. There were a couple of things she said which led Jenny to believe she had some psychic powers.

Della knew that she was born in November like her own mother. It was possible for this fact to have been obtained from hotel records. To guess, however, that Peter had a January birthday, that it had been a good partnership, and he had not been well for a few years, was harder to explain logically. As Jenny had her face down, she could not have seen the tears. When she was about to ask her to stop, a change of subject came about so it was said not to upset her too much.

Afterwards, when it came to the blow dry, she felt that there was more she could have been told.

What will be, will be, she thought, especially regarding how the evening would be played out. That was to come, her interest, at that moment, was her hair and the style that would ensue. It was different, but it pleased her. Even so, she yearned for Peter to be there to comment. Would they both have been going out this evening? she wondered in returning to her room. Rik had never met Peter and she doubted if he would have wanted to make the acquaintance of the new Señor Carballo. Such were her thoughts in making her way back to her room.

CHAPTER 10

Promptly at 6.30 p.m., a smart taxi driven by a very courteous fair skinned Cuban, who spoke good English, arrived to collect her. Sitting alone in the back of the car and 'all dolled up', she felt confident and good about herself.

If my friends could see me now, she thought and that song from 'Sweet Charity' lingered in her mind as they drove through the suburb of Miramar, with its villas built by the rich in pre-revolutionary times. With many having become embassies, or the property of large companies, the area still had a privileged feel. Sadly, reaching the seafront called the 'Malecon', a contrast was noticeable. The breakwater needed repair and many of the older buildings needed some TLC, not that this mattered to the youngsters who congregated on the sea wall, while families promenaded as the sun set.

Jenny's destination was the renowned Hotel Nacional de Cuba at which, in the 1930s, when a Hilton Hotel, the rich and famous had stayed. Film stars like Ava Gardner, Frank Sinatra, Marlon Brando, Errol Flynn. Even politicians like Winston Churchill had been a guest. Her hope was that there would be an opportunity to savour the ambience of the hotel, especially to peek in to its dining room, reputedly stunning. Alas, she was to be disappointed. During her visit she had no opportunity to satisfy her curiosity.

On arrival, she was escorted, by a young porter, to a small function room on the first floor, the venue for the private party. He had been clearly tasked to meet her which foiled her intention to explore before declaring her presence. Entering the room, she was immediately aware her arrival completed the group. Rita greeted her as if a friend of long standing and quickly, charmingly went through the ritual of introductions, tasking her brother Leon to ensure Jenny was looked after.

Rita looked very stylish. There was an allure about her which was an asset she knew how to use. Indeed, she and Rik would probably be described as quite a distinguished couple who certainly seemed happy together. Yet, in the old days, she would not have been Rik's type being much too self-assured and confident.

Might it be that Rita had ensnared him? She wondered if she might be a lady spider, who...?

Reprimanding herself on her overactive imagination, she became aware that a waiter was offering her a 'mojito' of which everyone had a glass, while a waitress was circulating with delicious canapés.

Rik was calling for silence, after which he asked all to raise their glasses to his beautiful wife, the evening's hostess, who would tell them the reason for the little get together.

"To Rita and thank you," everyone chorused.

Rita began by introducing herself as Marguerita Rosita Carballo, a very Spanish name wherein there was a clue to what she was to go on to say. Firstly, however, she thanked Rik, or her Ricardo, for being so understanding of her wish to keep her maiden name, a name she had clung to in previous marriages also. Like Rik, she had been married before and sadly widowed. Both were convinced that the third time for both would be extra special and lots of years would follow as good as their first.

"A toast to Rita and Ricardo," was proposed by Max, one of the Canadians and glasses were raised with the waiter discreetly offering further drinks to those whose glasses were empty.

Rita went on to explain that the trip to Cuba was a fiftieth birthday present, for, in 1960, she had been born in Havana. When a year old, however, her parents escaped to Florida leaving all behind them. Still, through hard work, they had become prosperous and when financial pressures eased, her brothers were born. Both were successful attorneys and were present to enjoy the celebration.

Her search for relatives had not been successful, but many people did 'disappear' following the Revolution in Cuba. She had seen where her parents used to live and the ruins of her maternal grandparents' place near Vinales.

It was big Gus, the older brother, there with his wife Lucy who spoke next. He was a six foot four inches hunk of a man with the physique of an American Football player whose deep voice was musical to the ear. What he wished to add were words of praise for their parents, their courage and hard work, and for instilling in them all the will to succeed.

Respectively, ten and fifteen years younger than sister Rita, he and Leon had been brought up somewhat differently, more American, despite their Spanish names of Augustin and Leoncio. They adored Rita whose travels and overseas residence, had taken her away from them more than their parents would have wished. During their student days, she had been very generous to them, but it was in her nature to be bountiful.

A momentary lull in the chat was broken by Gillian who reminded Rik of his promise to tell them about his rings – which they so adored. Taken aback, and hesitant in responding, Jenny suddenly realised that this was a good opportunity to seek a reaction. Maybe she thought, she was emboldened unwisely by the two mojitos drunk.

"Oh please, let me guess," she implored excitedly acting as if it was a game. "Wait a minute I have just a way to give an answer," whereupon she took out of her bag a small rounded crystal, which she asked Leon to hold on the palm of his hand.

Continuing the charade, imitating as best as she could, the actions of a seer, she looked into the crystal.

"They have an interesting history, especially since coming into your family two hundred years ago – I'm waiting for the mist to clear from their past... Now I see an accident... two men dead... debris... a plane perhaps... People around are black. Is it South Africa?"

To redeem the situation, if she had gone too far, and to lighten things, she laughed. Before quickly adding that if she was a writer, that would be the background to her story. Then, unlike Rik, the inheritor of the rings would be an arrogant man to whom women were mere toys to be dispensed with when he was bored of their company.

Fortunately, all seemed to have accepted her performance as a piece of fun, that is, except for Rik who was staring at Jenny. Consequently, he did not hear Gillian laughingly say that he could not cap the fantasy just heard, so to forget her request. Then, having regained his composure and with the others talking amongst themselves, he approached Jenny who was putting away her crystal bauble.

"Your imagination is such, Jenny Moran, you should write a book and, of course, dedicate it to Rik."

"Sorry to disappoint, she replied, "my dedication would be to..."

"Peter," he interrupted.

"No," she retorted sharply. "It would have to be Laura Fuller."

If he was taken aback, or unsettled in any way, there was no visual indication and the waiter's request for all to take their seats deflected his attention.

Leon did whisper the question, "What was that all about? You'll have to tell me."

Both held back, allowing the others to seat themselves where decorated name tags directed.

The table was round and moving clockwise from

Rita, people sat as follows: Gus, Lucy, Leon, Jenny, John, Elaine, Max, Gillian, Rik. During the meal, conversation flowed easily and, for the most part, was inclusive of all. No one dominated, but most of the hilarity was created by Max. Even Rik seemed relaxed, though Jenny felt sure he was noting her every word and gesture. He need not have worried, she was determined to enjoy herself: the food was excellent, so was the wine and Leon was very attentive.

Before coffee, a comfort break was suggested. The powder room adjoined the suite, so again no opportunity for Jenny to explore. The talk amongst the women was about fashion, hairstyles, make-up, to the delight of Lucy, Gus' wife, who came into her own. To her, it was an anathema that Jenny merely powdered her nose and put on lipstick. She insisted that Jenny removed her glasses while she highlighted her blue eyes with an eyeliner and mascara she had in her bag. Jenny might not have designer labels, but she always looked smart, her hairstyle suited her, but make-up, she did neglect.

The ladies emerged to be greeted, in fun, by various comments on the time taken. Rik, John and Gus had decided that as they were in Cuba, a cigar was in order with the distinctive aroma already noticeable. The coffee, too, smelt inviting and was no ordinary brand. A photographer arrived, along with four musicians who were to play for listening and dancing. Rita announced that she would allow no one not to join in, especially as she wanted to dance with each of her brothers and did not want anyone to feel neglected. She and Rik then took to the floor with everyone soon following.

When Rita danced with Leon, Rik danced with Jenny, giving him a chance to tell her that she seemed to have mistaken him for someone else. When she disagreed, his hold tightened. The nasty scarring on his left palm had left her in no doubt of his identity. Any tension was well disguised by both and straight afterwards a conga brought to an end the dancing session. Jenny was prepared to leave, until told her taxi back had been booked for 11.30 p.m.

The musicians were good and it was lovely to sit and listen when they started playing again. There was no denying that everyone was pleasantly relaxed. Jenny went to speak to the Canadians and wish them well, they were leaving on the Monday. Max gave her a business card for he and John were in partnership running a clinic, their speciality being cosmetic dentistry. Elaine and Gillian, she felt, would have liked a quiet gossip but had to content themselves with general pleasantries.

When dancing, Leon had asked her to meet him the following day, Sunday. Then, a while later, he had whispered a taxi would pick her up at 10 a.m. and it would drive them to Cojimar, and they could talk. All this had been arranged in a very surreptitious manner. Thus, when Rita insisted on having her home address to which to send the photographs in case they could not drop them off at the marina on Thursday, Leon felt free to casually say:

"Hope to see you soon, then."

It was Rik who accompanied her when leaving. The

lift was empty and, once the doors were closed, she felt compelled to challenge his conceit and smugness.

"Richard Heston, Houghton, Van Hooten, or van Huyten, so many aliases, but always the rings. Married more than three times and, sadly, one of your wives was Laura Fuller. Her sudden death, like those of others, raised questions."

With just one floor to descend, she had no time to say any more. On stepping out, he directed her to an empty settee in the lobby and quite calmly bid her to continue.

Her thoughts were racing: she was unprepared and was she mad to declare her knowledge? "You have been very clever," she said quite calmly. "Not too greedy, no insurance policies to heighten suspicion. To you, women are just toys, of fleeting interest and dispensable. Has it become a game which you always win?"

"Go on," he urged, when she hesitated a moment.

"Rita is more self-possessed than the others. Maybe at 65, you are thinking of retiring before your luck runs out."

"The others, tell me about them," he asked sneeringly.

Ignoring the comment, she tried to goad him. "Surely, you want someone to know how very, very clever you have been?" Suddenly, something dawned. "That is why you wear those distinctive rings, to remind yourself of your genius which others always fail to see. They are your talisman, as in the legend."

He clapped. "Jenny Moran, I like your imagination, audacity, courage even in challenging your Rik van

Huyten, that is, if I *were* him. Let me get you into your taxi where you can imagine some more."

'Ouch,' Jenny thought as they made their way to her taxi parked near the doorway. 'Too late for regrets,' and she did not feel apologetic. Nor had she expected a confession. All she wanted, or hoped for, was to dent his assumption of infallibility, an impossibility perhaps.

When she was seated and before closing the door, he bent and whispered in her ear. "If you write the story, make the number seven."

The door slammed and the taxi drove away. The driver engaged in polite conversation, but her thoughts were elsewhere.

CHAPTER 11

Back in the solitude of her room, just after the bewitching hour of midnight, she was tired, but not sleepy. A coffee at the poolside bar was tempting – it was open 24 hours – but she knew the caffeine would keep her awake. Never a good sleeper, from looking at the clock as the darkness slowly ticked away, Jenny was very aware that she was snatching sleep only for a few minutes at a time.

Her mind was active, going over her action in confronting Rik. What had she gained? *Nothing.*

Others had challenged him in the past, to their cost. Some, in vain, of which she was one now. Laura Fuller was more of an acquaintance than a friend, but she had been fond of Laura's mother, Margaret, also a victim and through whose urging she had become introduced to Rik. Then, there was that chance encounter with the South African, Mark Grosman, whose allegations first pointed the finger with his warnings coming too late.

What would Leon make of all she had to tell, she wondered? He was the only one to sense that her act with the crystal was not just fun. Maybe everyone else was too polite to embarrass her by commenting. Her action had not thrown any dark cloud over the occasion. Rita's warmth towards her had not cooled.

However hard she tried to distract her thoughts and get some sleep, her efforts continued to fail. When the clock finally ticked its way to 6.30 a.m., she decided to get up and go for a swim. Her twenty minutes exercise invigorated her and made her in the mood for breakfast. The restaurant, when she got there around 7.20 p.m. was empty. Not until she was leaving did anyone else appear. A group of ten, she guessed Cubans, there on one of the weekend package deals.

It was Sunday morning and, when she sauntered back to her room, the lack of movement did indicate it was being taken as a day of rest, or at least early morning rest. Without doubt, the quiet calm would not last long. To her surprise, the room maid was leaving her room as she arrived. A tidy person, the maid's task was easily accomplished. Indeed, Jenny's halo glowed as she thought of the state of some rooms she had glimpsed, in passing, in various hotels. Her sympathy for cleaners who had to tackle such rooms was always great.

Bringing her journal up to date, getting herself ready for the outing ahead, soon brought the time to 9.30 a.m., when she thought she would wander towards reception and see if there was anyone with whom she could chat. Helen was settling herself on a lounger, armed with her iPod, yet she was eager to inquire where Jenny had been going to, by taxi, the previous evening. There had been speculation until the Riveros were seen and whom Helen intimated were equally as intrigued by Jenny's absence.

Before Jenny could satisfy Helen's curiosity, the Fowlers stopped on their way to breakfast while one of the porters shouted: "Taxi for Mrs Moran."

Thus, all Jenny said was that she was off to Cojimar and, hopefully, would see them later. Somewhat mischievously, she added that she would then tell them about 'The Old Man and the Sea'.

Yet another taxi and another driver, three days in a row, she had left the hotel in a cab. Pedro introduced himself, stating that his cousin had been the driver the previous evening and he had said:

"Mrs Moran is a very nice lady with rich friends."

So, he was honoured. His wish to ingratiate himself, she put down to his youth, early twenties. His English was good and he wanted to talk to become more fluent which would help his business ambitions. Very quickly, she was of the view that he would succeed at whatever he tried.

Leon was waiting for them on the Malecon, opposite the Monumento al Maine.

"Mr Carballo, very good looking," Pedro had remarked on pulling up to collect his passenger. Probably he was thinking, he was her 'toy boy', there being twenty years between them, though Jenny's looks belied her years. Anyway, a good looking escort did no harm to her image!

Both fell into easy conversation, beginning with her introducing Pedro, an opportunity to state that his English was excellent, and also that he was ambitious and knowledgeable. A wink from Leon indicated that he had understood the driver would be an avid listener.

Pedro advised that Cojimar was not far and so he suggested a stop at Playa del Estas would be worthwhile. The beach there was long and sandy and, being Sunday, lots of classic cars would be seen, which proved to be so. Yet, finding a quiet spot at which to park was still easy and Pedro had a lovely surprise in store. In the boot, he had a pump flask and all the necessary items to offer them a mug of coffee with a biscuit. Definitely, he had all the attributes to succeed and deserved to do so.

Jenny shook off her shoes, and, mug in hand, made her way to the water's edge. After some five minutes, Leon came onto the sands and indicated a walk. They fell into stride, an opportunity to get to know more about each other. Leon knew that she was widowed but little more, and she wanted to tell him about Peter and the loss she felt.

Following her lead, Leon revealed Mandy, his wife, was in Europe with their two children aged six and eight, visiting both sets of grandparents. Mandy was unhappy claiming his work dominated their relationship. His argument was that his hard work gave the family a comfortable life and security for the future, his aim being an early retirement.

What she heard saddened Jenny and she told him so. "You are not living your todays because of dreams of distant tomorrows."

All the money in the world would not buy back the yesterdays missed with the family. Sternly she continued, "To save your marriage you must act now. Go to Europe, after all, you did find time for Cuba."

Back in the car, Pedro inquired if they had enjoyed their walk. Almost in chorus, both thanked him for stopping, giving them the chance to take in the beauty, made all the better by his surprise of coffee. Clearly pleased, Pedro informed them that the best table at 'La Terraza' awaited them and they would be there very quickly.

What he then wished to know was whether they were avid fans of Ernest Hemingway and seemed relieved when both admitted that they knew slightly more about the man than his books, which was very little. To their surprise, he revealed that he had read many of his books without much pleasure, but he was happy that Hemingway's name attracted tourists. Graham Greene, who had shown a fascination with Cuba, also, he understood much better and he listed his favourites which included *The Third Man* and not unexpectedly *Our Man in Havana*.

Wow! Jenny thought, congratulating him on his reading.

Encouraged by this, Pedro went on to say he thought Greene a very clever man as he had written that there were Russian weapons hidden in the Cuban countryside, long before this became a reality in the 1960s. The man, he said, must have had a crystal ball. This made Jenny start giggling, much to the bemusement of Pedro, until a smiling Leon apologised, explaining that it was a private joke about crystal balls about which she was laughing.

CHAPTER 12

They arrived in Cojimar which, on reflection later, Jenny thought they had not paid attention to as was deserved. The fort, the bust of Hemingway, the harbour, the boats, had been seen but in a casual hurried way. Both wanted to talk about Rik and Rita. Thus, they merely glimpsed at all the photographs of Hemingway, which 'La Terraza' had in great number, being too eager to get to their table. Others, of various nationalities, were clearly on the trail of the 1954 Nobel Prize Winner for Literature. Any other time, it would have been interesting to eavesdrop on any opinions, expressed in English.

The restaurant was renowned for its fish and signature dish of paella, so they agreed on a small, fish starter with paella to follow. Beer was chosen, not wine, but Leon had to be assured it would be chilled; so typically American. With their order settled, Jenny asked Leon to start with his narrative of Rita whilst hers would explain her performance with the crystal.

Leon began by saying that he knew his sister mainly from a distance rather than closely because of the difference in age and Rita's domicile in Europe. A good linguist, he believed that she could have been successful in the academic world, or in business, had she so wished. For a while, he could not fathom Rita's lack of career in view of the strong work ethic their parents instilled in them. Then, by accident, he discovered the probable underlying reason.

Some years before, a congressman, he met through work, on hearing his surname, recalled a very bright student at Harvard when he was there called Rita Carballo, adding that she was also very striking. Indeed, a fellow student had fallen very heavily for her and pursued her relentlessly until she succumbed. Being the eldest son of 'East Coast Royalty', his family would never have allowed a marriage and he knew this. He knew, too, that he would never defy his family's wishes, their money being vital to his political ambitions. Still, he lusted after Rita.

"Nice fellow," Jenny interjected with a sneer.

"Worse to follow," Leon responded, continuing with his story.

Along with some five others, so the congressman recalled, Rita was persuaded to spend a vacation at a Californian hacienda owned by one of the parents. All were in the plot, construed by her suitor, to dupe Rita into a bogus marriage following her acceptance hesitantly of his proposal and great promises.

On their return to Harvard, the 'ardour' of her supposed husband cooled markedly. His excuse was that he needed to excel in his last year, and not being as clever as Rita, he had to work far harder and not be distracted.

Soon Rita discovered she was pregnant with twins which stirred things up especially as she refused to consider an abortion. It was likely that her refusal was driven by a need to frustrate her traitorous beau and his family, rather than religious reasons. No one wanted a scandal and it was avoided.

Rita did finish her studies 'cum laude', but she also gave birth by caesarean to twins, a boy and girl. A difficult labour necessitated surgery afterwards, hence no further children. Her twins were adopted by a childless cousin of the father while she received financial payment provided she headed for Europe.

Conveniently, at this point, the fish starter arrived, a succulent piece of white fish, lightly grilled, with a salsa dressing. Whatever, 'pescado' (fish) it was, there was the agreement that it was delicious and well filleted. Two more beers were ordered before the paella was presented in a cast iron dish from which they could serve themselves. The amount, in typical Cuban fashion, was generous.

Meanwhile, continuing his story, Leon explained that with her bounty Rita had bought a dilapidated castle near Salamanca in Spain whence it was thought the Carballo family came originally. Over the years, the place had been lovingly repaired and restored and put in trust for the family. It was there that their parents now mainly resided.

Probably on the rebound, and at a guess, enamoured by the idea of the title 'Duchesa' she married a young Spanish nobleman, making sure it was noted in the right

US magazines to be seen by the family who rejected her. Unfortunately, he was a womaniser, a spendthrift, arrogant with a cruel streak and very disappointed at Rita's lack of real fortune. It was not a marriage made in heaven. When he was killed in a riding accident, just two years into the marriage, Rita was accused of causing his death.

One of his mistresses, out riding with the couple on the fateful day, accused Rita of deliberately spooking her husband's very temperamental stallion as he was about to mount. He fell back, his foot caught in the stirrup and, when dragged, he hit his head against a stone pillar. The verdict was that his death was an accident, a very unfortunate mishap.

Within a year, Rita had married a French industrialist, a widower, thirty years her senior with two grown up sons. He absolutely adored and indulged her. When his health deteriorated, she was devastated, more so when he slipped quietly into a Swiss clinic to terminate his life. That was five years earlier, and Rita maintained that the idea had been planted by a greedy daughter-in-law not able to wait any longer for their inheritance.

It would seem that at the outset, Rita has insisted that all she would inherit would be her jewellery, personal paintings and the apartment in Paris. This had been a way of ensuring the sons never felt threatened by her. Of course, from generous housekeeping and personal allowance, she had been able to renovate and furnish her Spanish castle and accumulate enough for a very comfortable future.

The marriage to Rik had been a total surprise. Since 2006, her partner had been another French man whom, until his accident when water-skiing, he thought she would marry. Pierre was horrendously injured and another water skier killed. Rik was amongst the witnesses to this tragedy, being aboard a nearby launch. Clearly, he became acquainted with Rita through the tragic event – perhaps, a shoulder to cry on.

None of the 'uncomfortable' facts in Rita's life were known to his parents, nor to Gus. Following the congressman's revelations, he had confronted Rita with what he had heard. Thereafter, he had become a sort of confidante but he always sought someone to check on what he was told to be sure he advised her correctly and wisely, but not all was heeded.

"I was going to ask you how you knew so much."

Except to make some casual comment periodically to allow Leon to enjoy his food, she had listened quietly to his summary of Rita's life. She had been thinking hard about what she had heard but all she said aloud was, "Rita has led a very interesting life," though 'colourful' was what Jenny was actually thinking.

It was time for dessert, or 'pud' as she always described it, and she explained to Leon that she meant pudding in case he had not understood because earlier the word 'fortnight' had puzzled him. There was a fruit, with a jelly of its juices, she had tried previously, and seen served, which both ordered. It was then her turn to tell Leon what she knew of Richard Houghton, or Rik van Huyten, as he was known to her.

Laura Fuller was a contemporary at university, reading the same subject. Not living in the small Hall of Residence, it was through attending tutorials with the professor that she had got to know her. The other two in the tutorial, living in the same hall, disliked Laura greatly. In fact, she was without friends because she could be pompous and disdainful. 'Daddy', a Whitehall mandarin, had convinced her she was special. Certainly clever, she was no beauty, Yet, her lovely auburn hair drew attention.

At the end of tutorials, the other two always beat a hasty retreat which was how, after some initial coaxing, coffee together became a ritual. Surprising in fact as Jenny had not hesitated in pricking the pomposity, and slowly, Laura had relaxed, even shown some sense of fun.

Near the end of the second year, she met up with Laura who looked dreadful and clearly in pain. More or less accosting a lady about to get into her car, she begged her to take them to the hospital which the woman did, maybe because Laura looked so ill. It was a real emergency, Laura being soon in theatre having her appendix removed. Finding a number in Laura's purse, she managed to contact her mother, Margaret. She was a charming lady with whom, through this incident, she formed a bond which lasted until her sad and sudden death.

It was Margaret Fuller who had the money, standing and contacts which her husband, Andrew, so coveted to succeed, or so Jenny had been told. He was a very able man who never attained his ultimate ambition, mainly it was thought because he was so impatient and irascible. Furthermore, he lost a lot of money speculating on the stock market. Laura, however, wore tinted glasses where 'daddy' was concerned. With Laura as an ally, Margaret was side-lined, neither appreciating their need of her. This was why Margaret spent more and more time away from London, in a cottage near Cheltenham belonging to her brother.

After Post Graduate studies, Laura rejected academia and followed her father into Whitehall, living in the family home in Eaton Place. No man would have gained her father's approval, and before his death from a stroke, she had shown no interest. Later, accompanying her mother, very reluctantly, to some social event, she met Rik van Huyten. From the moment they met, Laura was mesmerised which Rik realised and encouraged. Within six weeks, he had moved into Eaton Place, invited by Laura, following his tale of being temporarily financially embarrassed due to the slow transfer of some funds.

How Margaret was to regret her powers of persuasion. Rik's charm did not enamour him to Margaret especially when he acted more like a master than a guest. He did not realise that the very valuable property was not part of the Fuller estate and would never be owned by Laura. It was Margaret's inheritance from her grandfather and many years previously she had put it in trust to her family relations. This was done most probably to prevent Andrew ever endangering it through his stock market ventures.

An urgent phone call had resulted in Jenny and Peter spending the weekend at Margaret's Cheltenham cottage, at which, from time to time, they did meet. Margaret's forlorn hope was that Jenny might be able to persuade Laura from doing anything rash. It had to seem somehow uncontrived.

Thus, Margaret was delighted to hear that Jenny would seek to manage something while in London for a conference in just a week's time.

On getting home, she posted a note to Laura with details of the conference, the hotel, phone numbers, explaining it would be good to meet, it had been a while. Not having received a response, at the end of the first day, Jenny decided to miss group discussions and try and catch Laura when leaving work. Her plan almost failed. Laura was leaving the building as her taxi drew up. Almost throwing the fare at the driver, she called out. Afterwards, she did think that Laura had hesitated somewhat before turning. That may have been because Rik was standing nearby with a taxi waiting. Anyway, the encounter did result in an invitation to join them for dinner the next evening.

"I've got wonderful news," Laura had whispered in kissing her before entering the taxi and departing.

CHAPTER 13

Coffee was served and Leon said he could guess at the wonderful news Laura was about to reveal. What he could not guess at was what she was going to reveal about Rik.

"So to continue," she said.

"When Laura's taxi had disappeared, she had stood transfixed until she heard the following:

"You look as if you have had a shock." The remark had been made by a tall, bespectacled man in his early forties, who continued, "Sorry, I am Mark Grosman and, *please*, if you are a friend of Laura Fuller, would you have a drink with me, or coffee if you prefer. I truly need to speak to you. It is important, crucial to your friend."

How could she refuse? Unfortunately, she had a feeling whatever he was going to say was to be too late. Walking briskly, they had headed to The Strand and found a bar which was not overly busy. Mark Grosman was a South African, his accent made that clear. Rikard van Hooten had eloped and married his young, naïve eighteen-year-old sister. Rumour had it that he was a young man who had gone wrong, no one knew why, or in what way. All that was known actually was that his father had disinherited him. Even when his father and brother died in a small plane crash, all Rik got were the two rings.

For a year, the marriage seemed to work. An import and export business set up by Rik appeared successful and with the income from his wife's trust fund, they lived well.

Returning from a party, they were viciously attacked and their place ransacked. His sister, Zara, had confided in him that, although she had not been raped, she believed Rik viewed her afterwards as 'contaminated'. It hit her hard but, by six months later, she had grown up. In fact, that was what she said to him on the morning of the day she died.

Alone, Rik having gone off to play golf, she had phoned Mark urgently begging him to join her for coffee, then lunch. Hastily, he hurried over. Quite calmly, Laura had told him she was going to divorce Rik and that she had invited his mistress, her supposed friend, over later to be told the news. In preparation, she had put some vintage champagne on ice for the occasion having found it in Rik's closet when prying. After all, she had added with a wry smile: 'It must have been meant for one, or other, of us'.

He left her happy, full of plans for the future and without any regrets. Later, about mid-evening, Rik had rung to say he had come home and found Zara, and Natasha, dead, he believed poisoned. He had phoned the police.

Here Leon interjected that any case against Rik would have been circumstantial, to which Jenny nodded. Quite correct, it had been concluded that Rik was in no way responsible. His explanation, throughout, had been that the poisoned champagne bottle had been left by the intruders and somehow overlooked. The verdict, however, had been that Zara was responsible, murdering her friend and taking her own life.

With the marriage just under two years in length, Rik did not gain financially from Zara's trust. Some months later, those responsible for the attack on both were caught. They admitted the assault, and break-in, stating it had been a mistake, the intended victims were to have been neighbours. Adamantly, they denied any knowledge of poisoned champagne which convinced Mark of Rik's guilt.

The question he then faced: 'Where was he?'

Some time later, a chance remark by a business colleague set him on the trail again. The throwaway remark had been that scandal amongst Kenya's 'Happy Valley set' seemed to continue. The chap had recounted that during a recent visit to family in Kenya, chat at 'The Club' had been about the recent death by poisoning of Lady Cynthia Seymour and her niece, Caroline Houghton.

The former had quite a reputation for her excesses, while her niece, whose guardian she had become, was a beautiful, but very fragile soul. Schooled in Switzerland, she knew nothing of her wayward aunt until she arrived in Kenya and then she tasked her to reform. The surprise came when Caroline married her aunt's lover, Richard Houghton. All sort of reasons why were offered in the gossip which circulated.

Outwardly, both aunt and niece, had remained on good terms, though it had been noticed that her aunt's excesses had increased while the niece seemed to be getting more fragile. Post mortem showed that both were being poisoned in small doses over a period of time, with that in the champagne being the finale. Out of jealously, it was concluded each had been poisoning the other. Any suspicion of the distraught husband was dismissed summarily, most people never seemingly doubting his shock, grief and innocence in what had happened. A few more sceptical surmised that it was not grief which led to his move to Zambia very soon afterwards.

By mentioning the rings, Mark had confirmed Richard Houghton and Rikard van Hooten were one and the same. His attempts to trace him in Zambia failed. Time and money had prevented any real investigation in spite of a rumour he had heard. Over the years, his own conviction of Rik's guilt had grown.

Imagine his disbelief when, on a business trip to London, he glimpsed Rik at the Grosvenor Hotel.

"The rings," Leon whispered.

"Yes, those rings," Jenny confirmed.

It was a convenient place at which to stop and both took the opportunity to find the wash rooms. Only then did she appreciate how busy the place was, especially the bar area.

CHAPTER 14

Fresh coffee awaited them at the table when they returned and Leon had taken the opportunity, during the interlude, to settle the bill. There was much more Jenny had to tell and Leon was eager to be told all she knew.

The sighting of Rik had prompted Mark Grosman to follow him and this had led him to Eaton Place. After this he hired a private detective who told him of Laura. His attempts to try and speak to her were futile. Rik was always around and he failed to get an appointment to see her at work. Thus, his plea to Jenny had been to warn Laura and get her to break with Rik van Huyten. It was then that Jenny had told him, Margaret, Laura's mother, had tried and she feared warnings were too late. Jenny told Mark she was sure Laura was wearing an engagement ring and wedding band. She believed it was the news Laura excitedly wanted to reveal to her over dinner the next evening.

Confirmation of this did come that following evening. They had not dined out; caterers had been hired to prepare and serve a most delicious menu which could not have been faulted, nor the choice of accompanying wines. It was meant to impress and did. When Laura declared she had never been happier, it was obviously undeniably true. Jenny accepted that her stressed statement that nobody was going to spoil things for her, alluded to her mother, and maybe to Jenny as well, if there at Margaret's behest.

Briefly, Jenny had been caught up in Laura's euphoria and her excited listing of future plans, a honeymoon, for instance. Rik had added that Laura would put her job and Whitehall behind her.

"Where will you live?" Jenny had ventured, coming to earth again and eager to hear what Rik might say. Immediately, he responded that they intended to sell the house along with its contents. She had felt that Laura was surprised.

Nevertheless, it was clear that neither appreciated that it was not theirs to sell, a fact she had nearly blurted out. The truth would be quite a shock, but it was not for her to reveal.

On returning to her hotel, she immediately phoned Margaret to tell her what she had gleaned, urging her to quickly return to London. Already Mark Grosman had phoned her, having been given the telephone number by Jenny. Both were to meet in London the next day before Mark's return to Cape Town. Other news was left until they met for dinner on the Thursday, the next day but one.

When she had phoned Peter afterwards, he had warned her to walk away from any further involvement. Sadly, both had feared, they were going to be on the side lines of some tragedy, which indeed proved to be so.

Margaret had returned to Eaton Place not to be well greeted by Rik, especially when he was told some uncomfortable facts. He was requested to leave, but guessing Laura would want to go with him, Margaret had rented for them an apartment in St Catherine's dock for six months. The house at Eaton Place had been offered to Margaret's twin nephews and their families, who were eager to make it their home.

Roughly seven months later, Laura had given up her job and bought a house near Woodstock in Oxfordshire. There had been a few phone calls and texts which had been a bit stilted. Then a text had come from Laura that she had booked them three days at a health spa, and Jenny must not refuse. It had been a complete surprise and not really convenient at short notice. Peter had expressed his unease at her acceptance and truthfully she had felt some strong doubts herself. The words 'imperative you accept' had been persuasive.

She learnt, on arriving at the spa, that Rik did not know the two were meeting. Thus, as Rik had insisted on driving Laura to and from the venue, Laura had arrived a day earlier and was leaving a day later. What was clear was that Laura was not very well. Never with much colour, her face was ashen, very reminiscent of that day, way back, when it had been necessary to rush her to A&E with appendicitis.

Before Jenny had time to say anything, Laura had rushed into a tearful explanation, namely that she was pregnant but was going to have an abortion as the foetus was not developing properly. Rik was ignorant of this and would have been very angry, not about the abortion, but that she had fallen pregnant.

All this had been poured out before Jenny had reached her allocated room. Once there, she had been glad to sit down to digest the information and whatever else was to follow. Having got the important news off her chest, Laura had begun to regain her usual composure. Until just a month previously, Rik's business enterprises had taken him abroad often on short trips, and then the time had been taken up by their move. Thus, Laura had been adamant that Rik had not guessed about her pregnancy.

The new house and its furnishings had been paid for by Laura, even though the place was in joint names. Emptying her account so considerably clearly had left her with more than a niggle. It did seem that her glasses were not as tinted as they had been. Usually not one to disclose her problems, worries or fears, it must have hurt Laura greatly to admit that there was so much about Rik she did not know. His business, for instance, which seemed to tie up his money constantly. Yet he knew everything about her financial standing, and about her life.

In a quiet aside, she had mumbled how her mother, on the day they left Eaton Place, had reminded her of the old adage 'marry in haste, repent at leisure'. There had been no contact afterwards between mother and daughter.

Leon interrupted Jenny's narrative at his point to ask, "What did Laura know about Rik's background? She must have gathered some information."

"That is what I said," Jenny had replied, "and I did ask her to fill me in, just to show that she knew more than she thought."

"Did she?" Leon was eager to learn more about his brother-in-law.

Jenny went on to tell him all that she remembered of what had been said.

According to Laura, he had been born and brought up in Namibia. His mother had died at his birth, hence his father's 'hatred' of him, while his step mother was more interested in her niece than in either Rik or his brother, who was older by ten years. Neither got on well, with the brother supposedly disliking young Rik equally as intensely as the father.

In such an environment, his rebellion is not really surprising and it did lead to his disinheritance. The father and brother died in a small plane crash, while Rik had gone on to make a living in the import and export business. He boasted that he was good at brokering deals but never elaborated. Finally, one interesting thing he had mentioned was that as a young boy, he had dreamt of becoming a pharmaceutical scientist.

This last bit of information, Leon thought was very important and significant. He admitted he had a lot of thoughts, as well as questions.

Resuming her account of the meeting at the health spa, Jenny recalled how Laura had informed her the abortion would take place the following day. Part of the mansion was also a clinic and well recommended. It was stated in quite a matter of fact way and yet Jenny knew that Laura had faced an emotional period alone, and in fear. Again whatever the repercussions, they would be faced alone as well, which had saddened her greatly. The worry and sadness had grown after Laura had undergone the procedure. She had appeared so drained physically and emotionally. What had been clear, the subject of the abortion was not to be mentioned ever again.

The massages and beauty treatments which had been booked for her, Jenny recalled that they had been tolerated rather than enjoyed as Laura's situation had never been far from her mind. More than ever, she had been glad to get home. The staff had assured her that Laura would be monitored carefully.

There had been no relaxation, however, on her return. Within an hour, the phone had rung with the news that Margaret Fuller, Laura's mother, had died very suddenly. Clearly shocked and distressed, Richard Villiers had asked if she and Peter could come and see him as soon as possible. They could stay at his sister's cottage, Mary Vine would be there, so they could contact her regarding arrangements. When they arrived the following evening, Friday, a distressed Mary had been very eager to talk and tell them all she knew.

The previous day, as was usual, she had been at the cottage, her day for cleaning and doing odd jobs. Margaret Fuller had been in fine form and, just a couple of weeks before, had undergone her annual private health check with pleasing results, Every Thursday, Margaret met a friend in Cheltenham for coffee and lunch at The Regency Hotel. Mary always drove her in, dropping her off at 11 o'clock and collecting her at 3.30 p.m. the ladies enjoyed their appetiser and wine. This was a well-established and timed routine.

In driving off, looking in her mirror, Mary had noticed a man near to Margaret. In fact, in meeting her friend, she had remarked that some 'down and out' had stumbled clumsily into her and worst still, she had been pricked, or stung by something, and showed a bruise on her foot. Within thirty minutes she had collapsed and a massive heart attack was suspected, which proved fatal.

"What did the autopsy reveal?" Leon butted in, not a surprising question from an attorney.

Jenny's voice, in replying, revealed her continued unease that nothing untoward had been found. Richard Villiers could not believe the result and was shattered by it and what was to follow. For the sake of appearance, it was agreed that Laura should be told, rather than to learn the news in another way. Jenny had revealed to Richard that Laura had just undergone an abortion for medical reasons, as a result, he had wanted Jenny to drive over to Oxfordshire to break the news to her. She had refused, however, feeling the news should come from her uncle, or another family member. So, the news was given very matter of factly over the phone. Richard had never liked his niece, Laura and her marriage to Rik had not pleased him, nor the way they treated Margaret thereafter.

Jenny revealed that she considered her refusal to go and see Laura a misjudgement, especially in view of what happened afterwards. According to Rik's later evidence, on receiving this news, Laura had become very distressed and insistent that she had to drive over to Cheltenham immediately, and not the following day. All arguments to the contrary, it was said had just worsened her emotional state. Thus, Rik said he had agreed to drive her, and that while she packed, he would book a hotel for them.

While he was phoning a hotel, Laura somehow tripped down the stairs. The receptionist testified that she had heard some bumping sound and Rik giving an anguished gasp that his wife had fallen down the whole flight. There was no broken neck and nothing else untoward was found during the post mortem. It was concluded the shock after her recent medical treatment had resulted in dizziness causing the fall which in turn brought about a heart seizure.

Rik was questioned several times, but the coroner's verdict that the death was a tragic accident remained. The abortion, the shock of her mother's death, the fall, had strained her heart far too much. Yet a detective had stated that there was something about Laura's packed case which niggled him. It also concerned him that 'everything was too clinical'. In addition, Rik's alibi for when Margaret had died was too convenient. It was corroborated by a neighbour, known for her affairs, who had looked in, concerned that Rik had complained of feeling poorly on the previous day. She had tried to phone but no reply so she called in and entered via the back door to find Rik in bed asleep. The phone had rung as she was looking into the darkened room and so she had gone to that on the landing to answer it and take a message. Mid-afternoon she had called again and found

Rik up and feeling much better.

Richard Villiers and Jenny had spoken to the detective about their strong suspicion that mother and daughter had been poisoned. They had managed to ascertain that amongst Laura's bruises, there was a puncture mark which had nothing to do with her operation. Not all the bruises came from the fall. Some indicated that she had been held firmly. Rik had admitted he had done so to try and calm her down from her hysteria. In evidence, he had stated that Laura had been devastated at the realisation that she would never be able to patch up recent differences with her mother, which he maintained was a mere blip in an otherwise very loving relationship.

For the sake of appearances, and the family name, Laura's uncle wanted nothing said publically: that what was believed should stay private especially as no proof only suspicions could be presented. Unfortunately, Margaret and Laura had been cremated, their ashes placed in a family vault with Laura's surname recorded as Fuller. Jenny had been advised not to attend the funeral service. Soon after, Rik sold up and left no forwarding address.

Rita had asked Jenny if she was familiar with the Ullapool area in Scotland where Rik had some property still to sell. This he had inherited from his wife Catherine who had died in 2005. It would seem she had long been an invalid, hence why they had lived mainly in Malta, the better climate. Just where in Malta, Rita could not remember which was a pity as she knew the island well.

Anyway, poor Catherine must be number 'seven'.

The number 'seven' was repeated by an aghast Leon. To explain how she was so positive this was the toll, Jenny told him she had challenged Rik when he escorted her to the taxi. Not surprisingly, he had denied her accusations but had whispered that she should make the number seven in any novel she wrote.

"A joke?" Leon had feebly ventured but like Jenny he did not believe this to be so, and that Rik had wanted someone to know how very clever he was at getting away with murder. It was a word she had tried to avoid for Leon's sake.

Exceedingly glad to have got everything off her chest, even if it meant loading someone else with a lot of uncomfortable facts, rumbled out at speed, all she wanted afterwards was to forget all about Rik van Huyten. Just a glance at Leon's face showed that he was very troubled, quite naturally, at what he had been told.

"I know there are loads of questions you would like to ask. We could discuss the matter ad infinitum, particularly, 'what now?' or 'what next?' but please let's change the subject."

Whilst making her desperate plea, she had given him a card with her home address and telephone number along with similar details for Richard Villiers and Mark Grosman.

Time had passed but it was not as late in the afternoon as Jenny had thought. Consequently when leaving 'La Terazza', she suggested a brief stop again at Playa del Este for a walk to clear the head. The plan was approved by Pedro whom they found having a siesta in his car.

He was interested to know what other parts of Cuba they hoped to visit. All the Carballos were to head for Trinidad the following day. Otherwise for Leon, Gus and Lucy that would be all their travelling. Jenny admitted that, maybe foolhardily, she was booked on a marathon excursion on the Tuesday to Santa Clara, Cienfuegos and Trinidad. This meant a 4 a.m. rise to be collected at 4.30 a.m. The very early start had made both men gasp, while Pedro wondered why she had not been joining Leon on his trip.

"Wish you were," had been Leon's response and, in different circumstances, she would have agreed.

The opportunity to tell them that she was going to the Club Tropicana on Wednesday evening was lost. They had arrived at Playa del Este. There were fewer cars and people than in the morning, but the sound of the sea was soothing as they walked. It was just the place to forget worries, and woes, at least for a while. There was silence; some light banter instigated by Jenny who offered Leon a 'cent' for his thoughts.

Suddenly, when walking back to the car, she issued a challenge of a sprint but, as she began running, she tripped. Being a gentleman, Leon came up to help her, after which she mischievously began to limp. Thus, thinking her challenge over, Leon fell into step alongside. Naughtily, however, when within a few paces of the vehicle, Jenny rushed to touch it first and declare herself the winner.

"Cheat," had been the cry from Leon with Pedro in agreement.

At least, it had infected a pleasant sense of fun as they headed back to Havana. Near his dropping off point, Leon had got her to agree to meet him at the Hotel Ambos Mundos at 10 a.m. on Thursday morning for an update on his thoughts. Her argument that she would use the hotel's courtesy bus into town was overruled, or afterwards that she would pay for her own taxi. Pedro's eavesdropping put paid to that as he offered his services, special rate for Mr Carballo. So a 9 a.m. pick up was agreed with a 1 p.m. return.

After Leon's departure, and on their journey to Marina, Pedro was full of praises for the generous Leon while cleverly trying to fish for information, not that any was given. There was agreement that Leon was not just good looking but a genuinely nice person as well. At the same time, Jenny was thinking that her holiday was being hi-jacked by circumstances. Still, she had been thinking that on Thursday, she would wander around Havana at leisure.

After dinner, she joined her compatriots for coffee at the pool bar. Helen was absent and had been seen only briefly early morning. It was hyperactive Patsy who asked her where she had been all day, and where, the previous evening. Her return had been seen by Patsy when going to the Marina's disco, but without Delroy. The surprise to most, was that there was a disco which they then were told was mainly used by staff.

At 9.30 p.m., there was a show in the outdoor theatre

and they all took their seats in the front row. The dancers were mainly backing for the two male singers who had good voices. However, one had a habit of holding his crutch as he gyrated and belted forth. This was usual Jenny was told amongst young pop singers. To her, it was unseemly, so, along with the Crofts, she left after some fifteen minutes. Despite the volume of the music, Bob Croft had been falling to sleep, there were benefits, at times, to having to wear hearing aids. They could be switched off, or not worn!

CHAPTER 15

From daybreak, it was clear it was going to be a glorious day. In such a clime and setting, Jenny wondered how anyone could be glum. She was looking forward to not doing very much, just some swimming and an early walk to the 'El Viejo y El Mer'. Not forgotten was the task of getting the very elusive tour company representative, Tanya, to make an appearance. The lack of any contact by her, she considered appalling. Still, the Millers and others, in their predicament due to the volcanic cloud, had seen her only once and had concluded the job overwhelmed her – not the most encouraging of testimonials.

Following quite a long swim as the solitary occupant of the pool, she returned briefly to her room. Then, having changed and got some sterling from the safe, she set off in search of Jacinta. By this stage, most of the UK crowd had gathered on loungers around the pool. Helen had beckoned, eager to inform her that Vidal and son had left the previous afternoon. In response, it was pointed out that it was a hotel where people came and departed. Afterwards, Jenny regretted being so terse.

Finding Jacinta, Jenny confirmed her booking for Santa Clara, Cienguegos and Trinidad for the following day, Tuesday, and for Club Tropicana on Wednesday evening, duly paying the sum due in 'pesos convertible'. The early morning 4.30 a.m. pick-up was confirmed, along with the time of 8 p.m. for Wednesday evening. Then, Jenny explained that the others were very eager to see Tanya, and hoped she could contact her to get her to the hotel without further delay. Various telephone numbers were tried with no success, and messages were left, leaving poor Jacinta very embarrassed by the situation, and very angry.

Leaving her to continue seeking the elusive Pimpernel, named Tanya, Jenny set off on her walk. This time, when she reached 'El Viejo y El Mer', there were two large black limousines, with darkened glass, parked near the entrance. Beside each, two young men in suits stood, while at the entrance stood two blue shirted door men, not seen before. One of the suited men approached her, inquiring in Spanish, what the purpose of her visit was, stating the place was a clinic.

Somewhat taken aback, she stated, in Spanish, her purpose was to change money. In English, she repeated her purpose that she had been directed here before and there had been no problem. Her inquisitor accompanied her inside, pointing to the Bureau de Change to which one of the young girls from the reception desk came to deal with her transaction. Her English was not as good as the charming young woman she had dealt with on her previous visit.

It was not her imagination that her waiting escort was glad to see her depart, and she did not think it advisable to loiter in the vicinity by walking to the sea wall. Naturally, Jenny did wonder who it was that was visiting the clinic, needing an armed escort. Was one a decoy car? Alas, the answer, she knew would remain a mystery.

When she got to the sentry point at the entrance to the marina, a workman talking to the guard offered her a lift in the back of his buggy where the seat was clear and clean. It would have been churlish to have refused. Furthermore, it was getting very hot and it was later than she had appreciated, not that time mattered on this occasion.

Her return to the lobby to see Jacinta was timely as she was actually speaking to Tanya. In fact, she was handing the phone over to Rosa, the hotel's PR officer who clearly was in no mood for any procrastination. The result was that Tanya would be at the hotel at 4.30 p.m. Jenny volunteered to relay the message to the others and would express that their attendance was imperative.

All except Helen were still around the pool, so relaying the message was easy. All that could be hoped for was that Tanya would actually turn up. But Jenny was very optimistic.

While she was enjoying coffee over lunch, Lee asked to join her. Conversation was quite light hearted at first. Suddenly though, Lee's mood seemed to change and she became quite deep and serious. When she was asking Jenny what she knew of Confucius, she became distracted. A green suited, quite ugly Chinese man was beckoning. Whoever he was, Lee was certainly not pleased to see him, but excusing herself she did go over to join him.

Intrigued, Jenny lingered a while. Whatever the discussion between Lee and the stranger, it did not appear to be going well. Her attempt to leave was thwarted when he grabbed her arm, forcing her to resume her seat. Lee's visitor would not have needed make up to be cast as a villain, a snakehead member of a tong. For Lee's sake, she prayed she was wrong in judging 'the book by the cover'. People watching was interesting but easily imagination could run wild. Thus, chiding herself, Jenny went towards her room.

Again time seemed to have flown and Harriet and Bob were on their way to the pool area, having had their siesta. It was time for afternoon tea. They thanked Jenny for getting Tanya to visit as they were eager to know the arrangements for their return. The volcanic cloud was disrupting flights to Spain and they, like the others, had flown via Madrid. Jenny also gleaned that there was nasty weather generally in Europe, as well as in the States. Thus, they all agreed, full advantage had to be taken of the glorious weather especially so as the summer in Britain might again be disappointing.

By the time Jenny arrived in the lobby area, all had assembled and, just ten minutes later, Tanya finally arrived. What she had to say was really what she should have been telling people the morning after their arrival. Her general spiel delivered, she then began a sales talk on the excursions available. With no immediate takers, she said she would return the following day when details of return arrangements would be given.

The visit, as far as Jenny was concerned, had achieved little except in establishing the principle that tour company representatives should make themselves known to clients. A contact number, and her availability to deal with any problems, were other promises she was forced to give. When Jenny left, the others were trying hard to pin her down to give a definite time for her next promised visit, an early time being the group's preference.

A quick swim followed, after which she got herself ready for her pre-meal appetiser and dinner. Joining the others later, she urged them to visit Havana if only on the courtesy bus so as to have a look around. In addition, she advised that a trip to Vinales was worthwhile. To come all the way to Cuba and return a week later without seeing anything other than the hotel and marina seemed a very great shame. At ten o'clock, leaving the chat to continue, she bade goodnight. The following day would be a long one.

CHAPTER 16

Jenny woke at 3.30 a.m. in good spirits. It had been a short night. Tanya's phone call at 10.30 p.m. telling her she would be at the hotel at 9.30 a.m. in the morning had been an unwelcome interruption as she was nodding off. To pass the message on, she left a note at the pool bar when she went there for a toasted sandwich and coffee at 4 a.m. All was quiet, just herself and the two on duty.

Prompt at 4.30 a.m., the taxi came and took her to the Commodore Hotel where on the dot of 5 a.m. the coach arrived with its load of intrepid travellers for the day. Of the twenty aboard, only four young Japanese were awake, although for the two girls, it was only to change position. At least, Jenny thought, they will require English to be spoken for she doubted Mario spoke Japanese. In accompanying her to the coach, the guide for the trip, a tall, lean man, named Mario, had told her most aboard were Colombians. He had assured her that they were better time keepers than the Argentinians to which she had retorted, "Hallelujah!"

The coach sped on its way for the next hour with no one aboard breaking the silence, Mario clearly appreciating the wish for slumber by most passengers. It was after the comfort stop that he regarded the tour as starting. This was a twenty minute break at a petrol station with a café where those with breakfast boxes would be allowed to eat. Probably, like herself, fearing that the next comfort stop might be some time hence, Jenny and some eight others ignored the refreshments counter.

Mario ensured that no one lingered, the success of this marathon excursion depended on good time-keeping. He explained that his commentaries would be brief, but that he always welcomed questions. The Spanish group, being greater in number than the English speakers, were asked not to dominate his attention. With that said, he believed everyone would have an enjoyable and interesting day.

It was explained that Central Cuba consisted of five provinces, each focused on the main town bearing the same name, or a very similar one: the provinces were Camaguey, Ciego de Avila, Cienfuegos, Sancti Spiritus and Villa Clara. Usually tourists either speeded through the area, or ignored it completely. Two of the named provinces would be visited by stops in Santa Clara, Cienfuegos and Trinidad. All three cities were interesting landmarks in this flat, plain area which, until the collapse of the sugar-for-oil trade with Russia in the 1970s, had been the most important sugar cane growing region.

After this Mario's interjections en route were few: just some general facts or interesting anecdote wherein lay his strength. Consequently, most people seemed content to snooze while Jenny was happy to look out of the window at the passing countryside. There was always something to note, the size and state of dwellings, any activity human, or wildlife. The turkey vultures were dominant everywhere.

First stop was Santa Clara, a pleasant university city but, more importantly, for fans of the Revolution in Cuba, the site of the last resting place of Che Guevara. In the Plaza de la Revolución Ernesto Guevara, a large statue of Che, in battledress, can be seen. His mausoleum, and that of comrades who fell alongside in Bolivia in 1967, lies beneath. Their remains had been disinterred and brought from Bolivia to Cuba in 1997.

All this somewhat confused the four Japanese as did the fact that Eduardo Che Guevara de la Serna was an Argentinian and a doctor of medicine. A doctor and a revolutionary fighter, the dichotomy did not sit well with them. The Colombians, however, seemed very interested and would have liked to have stayed more than thirty minutes in the Mueso Historico de la Revolutión depicting Che's life and career. They were placated by a visit to Monumento a la Toma del Tren Blindado, namely the preserved four carriages of the troop train wherein Che and his men were ambushed in Santa Clara in January 1959 on a journey from Havana to Santiago.

As everyone climbed aboard to press on to Cienfuegos, there was great chatter amongst the Colombians. There had been plenty of smiles in the direction of Jenny and the Japanese but no one ventured to say anything in English. She and the young Japanese had exchanged pleasantries and comments. Their discussion about a doctor being a revolutionary continued, for they had told her the two young women considered a doctor's mission was to preserve life, while the two young men thought that Che was trying to improve the future for people. The health service established in Cuba, post revolution, made Che's efforts worthwhile, just one benefit. Jenny had smiled and responded with the age old question: 'When do ends justify the means?'

By the sound of their chatter as the coach sped on, the debate between the foursome continued. In nearing Cienfuegos, Mario was eager to tell them that the city would impress and to ignore the industrial suburbs through which they approached. Without doubt, the position, sat back in a large bay, was a feature. So, too, was the city centre with it pastel coloured neo-classical buildings near which they alighted from the coach. The Parque José Marti, it was stressed was the country's largest. It was very imposing. The monumental red domed building contained government offices. There was a brief guided tour of Teatro Tomás Terry, which was built in 1890, and named after a rich Venezuelan sugar plantation owner. The frescoed ceilings were lovely and the semi-circle of tiered boxes and the wooden seats were said to be largely original.

It was easy to imagine a well-dressed audience, the buzz as people awaited the start of performances, ladies using their fans, not only to cool themselves but to hide their gossiping remarks, or, if young, to shyly hide, following a smile from a flirtatious beau. Enrico Caruso and Sara Bernhardt had performed in the theatre which was still used. At weekends, it often played host to one of Cuba's top ballet companies.

Ten minutes was allowed for the Catedral de la Purisma Concepción, built in 1870, situated on the square's eastern side. Its interior was attractive and its twelve stained glass windows depicting the apostles were worth viewing. No one lingered. The next stop was that for lunch, a very attractive prospect to all: loudly cheered by the Colombians.

The drive, along the main thoroughfare and then along the Malecón, gave the opportunity to note some smart waterside villas with the Palacio de Valde and the Castillo de Jagua, on an island, being pointed out. Still, thoughts were on food and not sights, although the position of the restaurant did give a good view of the bay, and they were reminded that the sea beyond was the Caribbean.

Jenny was approached by Mario with the suggestion that he sat near her at lunch so that she would have someone with whom to talk. This, she thought, most considerate, and was very happy to accept. Consequently, they sat opposite each other at the long table prepared for the group. Beside them sat the Japanese and then the Colombians: the arrangement made everyone happy.

The menu was similar to that enjoyed on the Vinales trip, with everything cleared in all three courses with most choosing wine to wash it down. The musicians who serenaded the diners, harmonised well. Being able to chat to Mario made this, a much more pleasant interlude for Jenny, although the Japanese had made the occasional comment in English. They were an exceedingly polite foursome of young people. The Colombians, clearly revived, ended up singing a couple of songs along with the musicians, quite the makings of a choir.

In chatting, Jenny discovered that Mario had travelled outside of Cuba, representing the island in Judo. Part of him, he admitted had been tempted to seek asylum in Europe, but his heart and family were in Cuba. The continued American embargo annoyed him greatly, he felt it was unjustified. The increasing trade with China displeased him even more. It was known that some unscrupulous traders used the containers to smuggle illegals, not to stay in Cuba, but then to move on to the States. As he spoke, Jenny could not help thinking of the man in the green suit who had visited Lee.

Too soon, it was time to hasten on to Trinidad where she learnt all the Colombians were to remain overnight. En route, the coach passed the Jardin Botanico Soledad, Cuba's oldest botanical gardens. Well worth a visit, they were told, if time had permitted.

Jenny and the four Japanese were to be given thirty minutes to wander around the Plaza Mayor in Trinidad while the coach went to deposit the others at the hotel. All five concluded that this was too short a time in this world heritage city said to be the finest preserved colonial city in the whole of the Americas.

"So much to be photographed," had been the comment from the foursome who did not want Jenny to wander too far from them in case she got lost.

There was much to view just in the Plaza Mayor. There were painted railings, sculptures of greyhounds, fanciful urns, besides the colonial buildings to be admired. The church had become the Museo Romantico housing porcelain and furniture while the other two such establishments on the square featured relics of the indigenous tribesmen and slaves in one, and colonial architecture in the other.

The square was reasonably quiet, but a local couple, in passing by, did inform Jenny that the square was often far too busy with tour bus people to be really seen and appreciated. The best time was the early evening. The town of Trinidad, they added, had enough of interest to spend a week in the place and she felt that they were very right.

Boarding the coach to depart on the homeward journey, the couple waved enthusiastically as if seeing off an old friend. There was a new driver, and a lesser number for the return journey on which Mario stated no time would be wasted. Only one comfort stop was scheduled. All, he was sure, were sad to leave Trinidad, a feeling endorsed by the newcomers who, again, were from Latin America.

The coach returned towards Cienfuegos which it skirted and then headed for Aguada de Pasajeros where the autopista, or motorway, was joined. It was pointed out that to the left of the coach was the Zapata Peninsula on the shores of which was 'The Bay of Pigs' – site of the attempted invasion by the US in 1961.

Not too long afterwards came the ten minutes comfort stop, after which, with darkness falling, the driver put his foot down. The road was straight, traffic was light, enabling a good constant speed to be achieved. Except for the Cuban music playing softly, everyone was quiet. It had been an interesting day and, in a way, Jenny regretted not staying the night in Trinidad which led her to think about the Carballos' and to wonder if they, too, were staying the night at the Iberostar Grand Hotel in the city. If so, then she was happier to be travelling back.

It surprised her to be dropped off at the marina but this was welcome after a long day. It was 8.40 p.m., just time for a quick change before taking up her table at the restaurant booked for 9 p.m., half an hour before end of service. Only one table was occupied and she did not recall seeing the people there before.

When she was about to leave, Patsy turned up. The group had been wondering if she was back and there was so much for them to tell. The arrival of the musicians to play at the pool bar meant the gossip had to wait after all until the next day.

CHAPTER 17

At breakfast, on the Wednesday, Jenny was joined by the Fowlers, and Delroy Benson, none of whom were usually such early risers. The three, however, were going to Vinales, having been persuaded, so they said, by her advocacy of her trip. All had booked through Jacinta, a fact which had not gone down well with Tanya.

She had turned up at 9.30 a.m., the previous day, and found them all congregated by the pool. Very eager to sell excursions, she had been openly disappointed that her success had been limited to the Robinsons who had decided, after all, to venture out on the Vinales trip. The surprise was that they were not at breakfast, the pickup time was 8 o'clock. Before she asked, she learnt that Patsy, being more of a night owl, had decided not to go. Delroy confided that his wife had been taken aback that he was prepared to go without her.

Around 8 a.m., as she was about to take her usual morning swim, she saw a coach on the roadway outside the main reception. Delroy alighted and hastened towards her. The Robinsons were missing and the delay was not going down well. Then, the two were seen. Being short and rotund, it was hard for them to rush. They, too, were not pleased, their tickets stated 8.30 a.m. pick up. Jenny truly hoped, as the puffed and red-faced coupled climbed aboard, that the rest of the day improved for them.

When drying herself, Helen appeared very eager to relay the news Jenny had missed. No sooner settled in the shade with a coffee, they were joined by the Crofts, and then Patsy. Bob Croft remained very unsettled that Tanya still had not confirmed leaving arrangements. Their confidence in her had been further eroded. Tanya had got her sums wrong when dealing with the booking made by the Robinsons. Sooner, or later, they would learn that she had got the pickup time wrong as well, but Jenny refrained from adding to Bob's consternation with this information.

On the previous day, after Tanya's departure, Patsy had persuaded the Fowlers and the Robinsons to join her and Delroy on a trip to Havana via the one o'clock courtesy bus. Once there, the Bensons had been mistaken, almost immediately for Cubans. Taking advantage of this, Patsy had negotiated a very good deal for them all on a carriage ride around part of the city. The tour had taken an hour. Afterwards, as it was hot, the Robinsons had spent the remaining time at a rum factory, conveniently near the pickup point for the return courtesy bus at 4 p.m. They had cheekily joined a coach tour group!

Helen, foolishly, expressed her disapproval of such behaviour. Only Bob's sudden interjection about something quite unconnected, eased the situation, otherwise Patsy would have let rip. Quietly Harriet whispered to Jenny that his condition followed a brain operation. It was as if he was recalling a comment, or answer, he meant to express hours, or days, before.

After any excursion Jenny went to give her comments to Jacinta and so, before lunch, she went to recount her enjoyment of the previous day. Jacinta's desk, and that of Rosa, PR Officer, were side by side and the two appeared to be in some serious discussion which, on seeing Jenny, they disclosed to be about Tanya. They knew about her mistake in calculating, made worse by her reluctance to acknowledge it, and they knew of her failure to note the correct pick up time. Additionally, she had berated Jacinta for booking her clients. Thus, in view of everything, they had spoken to the Cuban Tourist Board which employed her.

During her late telephone call, on Monday evening, Tanya had told Jenny it was the isolated situation of the marina, away from her hotels in Havana which caused her difficulty. Relaying this, Jenny suggested that it might be pertinent to any review. She also added that she thought further training and support would not go amiss and that she would be saying so in her comments to the tour company back in the UK. The positives, in Tanya's favour, were that she was smart in appearance and her English was excellent.

Her postscript was that she had enjoyed her excursion. Mario had done a good job with his commentaries and keeping the group on time and happy. Jenny admitted that it had been foolish of her not to have joined the two day trip so as to see more of Trinidad which had impressed greatly.

Ready for her visit to the Tropicana, she had booked another massage and wash and blow dry. Although going alone, she was excited. How could she come to Cuba and not see the world famous cabaret? Della sensed her eager anticipation and assured her she would not be disappointed. Indeed, Della seemed especially pleased that Jenny was venturing forth and doing things to get to know the island. Her wish was that she would return, but it would not happen as Jenny had other places to see. This was not hard to surmise, but what of her prediction?

In telling that Sunday would be Mother's Day when the hotel would be very busy, Della had added that it was likely a travel offer would be made, an important one she said with a smile and wink. Jenny's laughing response had been: "All expenses paid, then yes, please!"

When leaving the salon, Della was eager for her to remember what had been predicted. For a moment, Jenny feared some unwelcome news about her homeward bound travel arrangements.

Joining the Crofts and Patsy for some tea, all she gathered was that the volcanic cloud continued to hover over Spain. Further conversation was halted: a magnificent very large yacht glided into view and moored directly opposite their table. Immediately, Patsy was urging Jenny to move to take photographs of her standing beside this beautiful seventy foot craft.

Owned by some film star, or pop idol, was Patsy's speculation and it really deflated her to see nothing flamboyant about the three on board. Away from the yacht, the three, two men and one woman in their thirties, at a guess, were very ordinary in both manner and dress. Paying no heed to the quickly gathered group of admirers, they moored and then left by taxi. All that had been learnt was that the accent overheard was Australian. Registered in Georgetown, Guyana, the boat's name *Maya Rea* reflected its grace and beauty.

Even the yachts Jenny had seen in Auckland in 2003, after the America's Cup were not in the same class. Everything about the vessel gave the impression it was new, very well-equipped and had cost megabucks. Patsy wanted photo after photo of herself beside the yacht and had to be discouraged from jumping aboard in her enthusiasm, with a reminder that it would be very well alarmed.

Suddenly Patsy's mood changed and a more serious side was revealed. The money, this boat cost, if given to a project like that for which she worked in London's East End would make an unbelievable difference. Its all-encompassing aim was to improve the lives and environment of poor families: it was a housing association, a save and lend bank, and it offered training. She worked encouraging people to avoid loan sharks, and counselling about debt. It became clear that Patsy was passionate about her work. Delroy and herself had better backgrounds. Her own father, now living back in Jamaica, had been an optician whilst Delroy's father had been a dentist.

Delroy was her second husband, her first marriage

had lasted only four years. Sadly, she admitted that in the last year, she had tried poor Delroy almost beyond endurance. Not going with him to Vinales had come about as he had said, the cost of The Tropicana, to which she wanted to go, was too high. If she was looking for sympathy, it was not forthcoming from Jenny. On the contrary, she advised Patsy to tell Delroy how she regretted not going with him and really to show interest when he told her about the day.

The group was dropped off, following the Vinales trip at 6.30 p.m., a good hour earlier than had been Jenny's drop off time. This was because there had been no stop in the town of Vinales itself. Even so the whole day had been a great success especially as the English speakers had been in the majority. The coach party had consisted of Canadian, British, Irish and East Europeans and there had been great hilarity. It was only Delroy, however, who had truly noted what he had seen and been told. Conversation at the pool bar later would be interesting and lively, of that, Jenny was in no doubt.

Prompt at 8 p.m. the taxi arrived to take Jenny to the Club Tropicana. The driver was accompanied by a Cuban tourist representative to deal with formalities on arrival. This helped greatly and gave the evening a smooth and worry free start amidst the bustle of arrivals, some not having pre-booked. Jenny was taken to the end table alongside the stage on the right-hand side. It sat six and those, who later joined, were two from the former East Germany, and three Venezuelans, and only the lady from Dresden spoke a few words of English. Conversation, however, did not matter, facial expressions clearly showed delight and enjoyment.

At exactly 9 o'clock, a quintet, smartly dressed in black, began to play classical pieces, and middle of the road romantic tunes. The group, consisting of two violinists, a cellist, guitarist and keyboard player, were a dream to listen to and could have kept the ever increasing audience in the open air arena, enrapt for longer than the allocated hour.

In a fanfare of sound and a blaze of colour, the cabaret began on the dot of ten o'clock. It was hard to know where to look, there were dancers, singers, musicians all around with tumbling waterfalls. The sheer scale of the spectacle was unbelievable. It was Rio Carnival, old Hollywood dancing spectaculars, all rolled into one. The singers, acrobats and dancers were all fantastic. The latter, scantily clad beautiful young women, had to balance impossibly large headdresses while performing. All the performers clearly wanted to entertain, their joy in what they were doing was obvious. The big song and dance production had to be seen, in the flesh, so to speak to appreciate the extravaganza. Words alone cannot convey the magic.

Leaving at midnight, carrying her untouched half bottle of rum, Jenny was exhilarated by the whole experience. Her waiting taxi driver read her thoughts.

"Not what you expect in a Communist country? Cuban, or Caribbean socialism, very different," he remarked as they moved off. That he was not a fan of the dictatorship under which the islanders lived soon became clear. It was time for change and more freedom than Raúl Castro had granted. According to him the regime had been stagnant for a long time. This was not the first time Jenny had heard such sentiments expressed. The dream of democracy promises so much to those who live in states without it, but is democracy always what it is cracked up to be? These were Jenny's thoughts, but journey time and the late hour precluded such in-depth discussion which she was sure the driver would have enjoyed.

Kindly, he dropped her off at the path leading to the stair well up to her room. Before reaching her door, she was startled by Patsy who was keen they had coffee together. It was 12.30 a.m. and Jenny, though not sleepy, was ready to rest. Telling Patsy to go ahead and order the coffee, she agreed to follow her very quickly. This she did and the two spent the next thirty minutes as solitary figures at the pool bar, Patsy agog to hear about the evening's show.

Having missed out on the Vinales trip which Delroy had enjoyed so much, she wanted to know if The Tropicana was worth the money and asking Delroy if she could go. Jenny truly believed Patsy would thoroughly enjoy the experience. However, she did not want to feel responsible if Patsy's enthusiasm caused discord between the couple.

CHAPTER 18

Another short night had been Jenny's thoughts on rising but that, when it was light and warm with another glorious day in prospect, the task was easier. Pedro, when he arrived at 9 a.m., was eager to know how her long day on Tuesday had gone. He also thought it a pity that her visit to Club Tropicana had been alone, not with a tall good looking escort. Fearful, too, that she might get lost, he gave her a map showing where he would drop her off and pick her up again, which Jenny asked to be 12.30 p.m. rather than one o'clock.

She was dropped off by the Museo Naciónal Palacio de Bellas Arte. Many of the fine prints in this gallery were left behind by families when they fled in 1959. Slowly she ambled towards the agreed meeting place and reached the Ambos Mundos ten minutes early just as Leon was arriving. In consequence, not ready for coffee, they wandered towards the Plaza de Armas to find a seat to sit and talk.

Suddenly, she was eager to find out what Leon, on reflection, thought should be their action with regard to Rik. Even so, she held back and asked about the excursion into central Cuba. With more time, two and a half days, they had seen the area at a much more leisurely pace. Again the city of Trinidad had made quite an impression and Leon greatly regretted that Jenny's time there had been so short – yet better than not seeing the place at all.

Each seemed hesitant to bring up the subject of Rik. Eventually, Jenny put Leon on the spot. His position was difficult, Rik was a family member by marriage. Still, she was in no doubt that the man in question was amoral and evil. Leon began by stating that he had watched Rik carefully whilst on their trip, during which he had been very pleasant, companiable and very attentive to Rita. Both had relaxed, and been at ease and very happy with each other, neither dominating.

Sharply, Jenny inquired if he was implying nothing should be done that his sister was happy and ignorance was bliss. Taken aback by Jenny's critical tone, he asked her to hear him out. Firstly, he had to stress that he did not doubt a word of what Jenny had told him, however much he wished none of it was true. The new Ricardo Carballo, alias Richard Houghton, Rik van Huyten, et cetera, were all one and the same person, and really not a very nice one. Naturally, he was concerned about his sister but, without tangible proof, telling her would achieve nothing.

Jenny's anger and frustration caused her to well up. It was the impotency of the situation which riled her. Hesitantly she began, "I know sinners are to be forgiven but only if they repent. Rik has not repented, Even if he had, could the fact that he wilfully took the lives of seven women be overlooked, or go unpunished? By knowing, do we actively condone?"

It was that which hurt so much, being complicit by association and it brought the tears flooding. What some passers-by thought, did bring a smile between them.

"Remember that I am on your side," Leon whispered. "You have lived with some uneasy knowledge for some fifteen years and now the frustration is compounded."

Jenny felt confused as well as frustrated. "Why did I have to bump into him again? Why did fate bring us all together? Will we solve that riddle?"

"Not here in Cuba, anyway," sighed Leon. "I promise you, though, once back in the States, I shall get a private investigator on the case. You will be kept posted. In the meantime, it is innocent until proven guilty. OK?"

"Of course," she agreed reluctantly, while remaining inwardly angry and frustrated. Yet, she knew that Leon was right in advising caution. Without tangible proof, there was nothing that could be done. The matter had to rest. "What do you want to do now? she asked, presuming they would not part company so soon.

"Mrs Moran, I shall be guided by you."

The word 'guided' led her, laughingly to assume the role of a guide, beginning by telling him all about the Plaza de Armas. One of her assets was an excellent memory. Her aim was to head off towards the Museo de la Revolución, having read it was fascinating, especially the section that dealt with the struggle for power. This, she thought, would be of particular interest to Leon. In addition, they would be able to see, outside the building, the 'Granma', the boat that took Castro and 81 others to Mexico in 1956.

When they got to the Plaza de Cathedral, they nearly bumped into Rita and Rik who were entering the cathedral building.

"Where are Gus and Lucy?" Jenny had inquired as they hurried on.

"Cojimar, a morning trip with others from the hotel," Leon replied, adding, "and, yes, they do know we were both there on Sunday."

"What about this morning?" Jenny feared that if Rik knew that they were meeting again, he would not be happy.

"No, I just said I was going to amble about the city. By the way, I should tell you that Rita has arranged for us to dine out at The Portofino this evening, a surprise for you."

This bit of news, explained Jacinta's request for her to be at reception at 5.30 p.m., stressing that the invitation extended just to herself. The reason given was for a chat with management which had not sounded convincing! "Thanks for telling me." Inwardly, Jenny had felt a bit disconcerted at the pretence that would be necessary. "I can do surprise, and I can do nice and charming, even to Rik. If he asks about Cojimar, I shall bore him with Hemingway. Should he ask, I shall assure him his secret is safe. I certainly do not want him to know that I have said anything to you." Jenny sensed Leon was relieved.

"For the moment, that's best, if you can make him believe you. Maybe, though, he'll have no chance to make any inquiries."

"Leon, don't worry, I shall be convincing, but let's forget the man. What do you think of Granma?"

The question took Leon aback for a minute, until Jenny pointed at the boat in a glass cage. Both laughed and agreed that the voyage to Mexico, for its passengers, would not have been comfortable. Besides the boat, there were other revolutionary relics outside the museum. A tractor, converted into a tank, and a delivery van used in 1957 in the attack on the presidential palace.

Having told Pedro to pick her up at 12.30 p.m., looking at her watch, Jenny said that she had an hour, to an hour and a quarter to spend inside but that Leon had no need to leave when she did. After all, his parents had lived through the struggle for power, some of his relatives had died or disappeared during the Revolution.

Both were moved by the blood-stained clothes, the worn, torn shoes and the heart rending, graphic pictures of torture, a mere glance at the pictures was enough for Jenny who felt physically sick at what was shown. Man's inhumanity to man throughout history was not something she could come to terms with, because as she tried to explain to Leon, every individual surely must have thought that they would not like to be the victim, yet it could happen if friends became enemies, or their power slipped away. Fortunately, Leon seemed to have understood what she was trying to say but was not expressing very well.

In fact, Leon agreed with her that there was never any justification for torture. However, he did believe that Revolutions even wars were necessary at times, and the aims of neither could not be achieved with the loss of lives. What he said reminded Jenny of the discussion about the Che Guevara between the four young Japanese. Although she asked him what he thought of a doctor being a Revolutionary, he was nor drawn into giving a reply.

Too soon, it was 12.10 p.m. Despite Jenny's argument to the contrary, Leon insisted on accompanying her to where Pedro was waiting to collect her for the return to the marina. Time spent in Havana had been far too brief. Yet, staying on was not an option, especially if she was to be surprised later by a visit from the Carballos.

Pedro's arrival was well timed and, on the journey back, he expressed his delight that they had taken time to visit the Museo de la Revolución, it showed they wanted to understand Cuba but he made no political comment. On arrival, he would take no payment or tip.

"Mr Carballo, very generous."

Thanking him and wishing him well for the future, Jenny was very surprised when, before he drove off, he said that he was sure they would meet again before she left the island.

After lunch, and before joining the others for coffee, she went to find Jacinta to be sure the 5.30 p.m. invitation had been just a ploy to get her to the reception area to greet her friends on their 'surprise' visit. This was indeed the case. Jacinta was disappointed, and puzzled, how she had found out. Assurance that there had been no leak on the part of the hotel, and that Jenny would act surprised seemed to satisfy.

Heading for the pool bar, she was met by Delroy who told her that Patsy was going to Club Tropicana which he had gathered Jenny had endorsed as spectacular. He added that he had relented without Pasty asking, so she was overjoyed. Not knowing their financial circumstances, she refrained from stating that it was a pity he was not accompanying her. In truth, her intuition was that it was a bit of tit for tat.

One piece of gossip that she gathered was that the Chinese gentleman in the green suit had visited again the previous evening. Lee and her Canadian college companion, had been chatting at the pool bar. They had not seen him arrive, and when she saw him, Lee got up to leave only to be grabbed by him to a tirade of Chinese. Lee wrenched herself free and ran off, while staff requested her unwanted visitor to leave. The puzzle was, what did he want? The group also, like herself, considered him very evil looking!

Leaving them to chat on and sunbathe some more, Jenny decided on a swim, then returned to her room. With all that was happening, it was harder than usual to keep up with her holiday journal. Yet, she felt, that it was more important than ever to recall as much as possible. It had been hard to drag herself from the pool in which she had been joined by Patsy whose excitement was so great that Jenny, prayed that the evening would live up to expectations. Truly though, she could not believe that Patsy would not be wowed.

Although sitting at the desk to write would have been easier, Jenny decided to sit on the balcony. Below her, the two aboard the Norwegian registered vessel had company, another two men. The remains of lunch still lay on the table and the bottle of wine, being enjoyed, was their fourth! If they came from Norway, then the cost of wine in Cuba, even though it came from Spain, was cheap in comparison to what they would pay at home.

A yacht quietly slipped by, and later, a large craft came in that must have been used, before conversion, for taking people on pleasure trips. It was hard for Jenny not to drift with her thoughts to the time Peter and herself had spent in Malta. Her parents, too, had greatly enjoyed the George Cross Island. They were happy days. It was good to have lovely memories, even if they gave rise to tears.

Even in the shade of the balcony, the air had reddened her skin more than expected. One spot on her back had to miss out on the cream, and it was her belief that no one could cream all their back themselves! What to wear, then took over her thoughts, a toss of a coin finally resolving her quandary. She remembered Lucy's advice and paid attention to her eyes. Pleased with how she looked, at 5.25 p.m., she left the room to make her way to reception.

At the bottom of the stairwell, she met the Robinsons who complimented her on her appearance. They, however, had overdone the sunbathing, not that they were concerned. Again they wanted to extol their trip to

Vinales and the fun all had enjoyed. It would mean a positive anecdote in their repertoire of stories.

In the foyer, the under manager and PR, Rosa, awaited, and, keeping up the pretence, informed Jenny they would be going over to the Piano Bar for that drink to which she had been invited. Both had to be complimented for their seemingly easy effort in keeping her engaged in conversation and ensuring she did not look outwards. Obviously Jacinta had not told them the surprise visit had been leaked.

Her dilemma, whether to tell them or not, was resolved when she heard footsteps behind her which were Rita's, the others a little distance behind. The exuberance of the friendly greetings overwhelmed her, brought tears in fact, that the element of surprise was taken for granted. In introducing the two management members, she jokingly admonished them for their part in the deception, while Rita turned to have a chat to them in Spanish, Jenny turned to the others laughingly stating that clearly they were there to see her new yacht.

"What?" Lucy exclaimed, for a moment taken in, then she hastily added, "What's keeping us? Let's go and look!" giving Jenny a wink.

Both Gus and Leon had gathered from Rita's Spanish conversation that The Piano Bar was open for the group.

Jenny was invited to lead the way during which they stopped to admire the boats in the marina, especially the *Maya Rea*. Even by Florida standards, this yacht was accepted as something special. The 'captain' of a lovely sea-going cruiser saluted them. He was dressed smartly in white and looked very professional.

Jenny explained that he was local and was awaiting the arrival of his American boss who came to use the boat for a fortnight each year. For that period, a person to cook and be a general deckhand would be employed and the boat would set out in search of big game fish.

They could have lingered longer, looking and chatting, but they were chivvied along by Rita and Rik, who had caught up with them. It was a jolly group which climbed the stairs to The Piano Bar where they found a lovely grand piano. The barman was ready with a tray of 'mojitos' to greet them, anything else would have seemed wrong. Rita noticed that Gus was eyeing the piano and urged him to try it out. Doing so, he showed that he was no mean player and Lucy clearly enjoyed his talent making several requests. To supplement his income while at law school, he had played in a jazz band. His light touch at the keys belied his physical largeness – he was talented. According to Leon and Rita, all the family's musical ability had been endowed only on Gus.

Conversation over drinks, and then over dinner at The Portofino flowed easily. A section of the small restaurant to the left of the door had been reserved for them and a screen provided complete privacy in the C-shaped room. The menu, with three choices for each course, delivered what it promised. Thus, there were deserved praises for the food and service, conveyed to the under manager. It made Jenny proud that the hotel had made such a good impression.

Coffee was served in The Piano Bar allowing a view

over the swimming pool shimmering with the lights, while the vista beyond of the boats, and then the sea, added that special ambience. Too soon, it was 9.30 p.m., and with Gus, Lucy and Leon on early flights to Miami, and Rita and Rik flying to Baracoa later, it was time for them to bid her goodnight. Rik's departing embrace did not have the warmth displayed by the others, nor did he endorse the 'hasta la vista', my new friend, expressed by Rita. Without a reminder from Leon, she would have forgotten to give Jenny the photographs which she had come to give.

Already having taken her seat in their large six-seater taxi, she handed them to Leon which allowed him to add an envelope and to whisper, in giving her one final hug. "I shall be in touch."

In a funny way, Jenny was sad to see them go, the evening had been so enjoyable. It was the last night for her group of compatriots, so she hurried to join them to assuage a feeling of emptiness. All were agog to know about her evening and who her friends were, the interrogation being led by Helen whose presence, she later gathered, had been a surprise to them. Disappointed that all she gleaned was that it stemmed from a chance encounter at Charles de Gaulle Airport in Paris and a dropped coat, she soon decided it was late and time for bed.

When she got out of earshot, it was the reserved Delroy who surprised them, by saying what they were thinking, namely that it was no wonder she was divorced. The hour, after all, was just ten o'clock. From Bob Croft she heard that two Scottish ladies had arrived, while two English couples were expected on Saturday. This meant that Jenny would not be without English company. They had all assumed a watching brief over her throughout the week to make sure she was alright.

Assuring them that this was good to know, she said that she doubted that the company they had provided would be replicated. She thanked them sincerely for the fun their company had been and it would be remembered.

The next hour passed pleasantly. Soon after eleven, however, the group called it a day. Jenny had thought they might have been tempted to stay and await Patsy's return from the Tropicana, but this was not suggested. Back in her room, Jenny glanced at the photographs and read Leon's note, a lovely positive end to the day.

CHAPTER 19

Usually when swimming, Jenny managed to detach herself from any serious thoughts, or worries. On this particular morning, this was not the case which she blamed on the fact that it was exceptionally quiet all around. If she had not breakfasted, she would have thought that she had mistaken the hour.

Her thoughts revolved around the previous evening. The conviviality, leading to much chat and laughter, had given little, or no time, to mentally dwell on Rik's past. In any case, the aim had been to have a pleasant evening, among new acquaintances 'friends' even, a term used by Rita several times. Even her note with the snaps was addressed to 'My Lovely New Friend'.

At least Rik was in the photographs. Some fifteen years before, Jenny recalled Laura, when they were at the health spa, regretting that she had no photographs of Rik, and would have to redress the matter. Mark Grosman had made the same observation that no snaps of Rik had been found amongst his sister's belongings. Did his inclusion, on this occasion, reflect the man's confidence that his past could no longer harm him?

Someone is innocent until proven guilty as Leon had stressed. This can be a salve to the conscience. Was this not the state of mind of those who were aware of atrocities, even by hearsay, but chose to ignore unpleasant truths? For such people, there was perhaps the excuse of fear and reprisal. Peter said she thought too deeply.

Getting out of the pool, she shook herself as much to get rid of her thoughts as to get rid of excess water before drying herself. It was then that Patsy bounded towards her. Even before she spoke, Jenny knew that the evening at The Tropicana had been a success. Unlike Jenny, Patsy had been picked up by a coach, aboard which were twenty-two others, five from the UK. All had thought the show stupendous, spectacular, the adjectives flowed.

Not surprisingly, Patsy had joined the show's dancers in their conga at the finale, and had gone on stage longing to dance the night away at the club. The shy Delroy would not have liked Patsy's exuberance. Yet, when he joined, he did say he regretted not going, which took Patsy aback. He added that he was glad Patsy had been with company, otherwise her excitement on returning would have been overwhelming. She had said that she had been tempted to come and knock on Jenny's door.

Delroy remarked that she had had a lucky escape, but his mood was light-hearted. He and Patsy left hand in hand for breakfast. This Jenny hoped was the beginning of better tolerance between them.

Aware that she would have the company of the group only for a few hours, Jenny had resolved not to wander far. Thus, she quickly returned to her room to change, after which she went in search of Jacinta to tell her how much the Carballos had enjoyed their visit and how complimentary they had been of the chef and service received. The comments delighted Jacinta. Staff were very proud of their place of work. To satisfy any speculation, Jenny let it be known that Rita's family had connections with Cuba in the past, hence her fluent Spanish.

Jacinta, she knew, would not have any antipathy towards those who escaped from Cuba. Not that Jenny knew, or had heard, of any Cubans harbouring such feelings. Many families after all, were sustained by money sent from relatives living abroad. Perhaps though, Jacinta's father might not have much time for those who prospered in the US, for it had been mentioned that he was an ardent supporter of Castro and the regime. In contrast, her mother, she had confided, was not so enthusiastic and grieved at having to keep her religious faith a secret. The fact that Jacinta, nor Jacinta's young daughter, had been christened concerned her greatly.

In telling her this, Jacinta had been keen to stress that Catholicism in Cuba was different. It accommodated many rituals and superstitions from the island's African slaves. For instance, pagan deities, 'orishas', had been partnered with a Catholic saint by taking on the character of that saint. This had originated as a way of disguising their own practices from their slave masters.

From her trips, and from talking to people, especially Jacinta, Jenny had learnt much about the island and this she valued. Before reaching her departing compatriots, she stopped at a table where two ladies were sitting and introduced herself. Their accents had given them away as being Scottish, although she learnt both now lived in Bristol and were work colleagues. Their holiday, on the island, had been delayed a month by the volcanic cloud, the eruption in Iceland happening only a couple of days before their original departure date. Both complimented the tour company for so quickly re-arranging everything.

The others had told them already about the shortcomings of Tanya, the tour company's representative, for those at the hotel. In their opinion, this was no problem, they would book their tours through Jacinta whom everybody had praised. They added that they were not intimidated by different environments, or using local means of transport, which they intended to do. Jenny refrained from mentioning the lengthy queues if they intended to use the local buses.

Another of their intentions was to use the beach in Havana for swimming. Their evenings would be taken up reading, being members of a book club back in Bristol. The brief conversation told Jenny a lot, particularly that there would be no late chats after dinner at the pool bar. Even her suggestion that they joined her and the others for a while was declined politely, but firmly. They had no time for idle chit-chat with people they would not meet again.

'That's me put in place,' she thought.

Hastening away, Jenny was greeted cheerily by the group. It was Patsy who put into words her thoughts about the two newcomers, namely that they were formidable, not the sort to allow anyone, or anything, to deflect them from their pre-ordained plans. Bob added that sadly Jenny could not expect any company. She assured him that with only a couple of days left, she would not feel too lonely. It would allow her to get to bed early and catch up on sleep. Even this did not allay his concern, and it was Harriet who stopped him going on, and thereby making Jenny feel very unsettled about the bleak prospect ahead as he saw it.

Surprisingly it was Helen who lightened the atmosphere by mentioning that there were to be shows on the next three evenings because the hotel was to be busy, the Sunday being Mother's Day. Already many families had arrived for the weekend by coach, taking up those package deal offers. More would come in on day passes. Thus, Jenny was advised to take up a seat, in the open air theatre area, early in order to get a good position. The advice was offered by Helen, in a friendly, concerned way, which surprised Jenny and, by the facial expressions, the others as well.

Chat amongst the group always flowed easily, no one dominated. This particular morning, there was an end of term feeling and, perhaps, at times, some nervous tension at the prospect of the flight and travelling that lay ahead. Future holiday plans, and possible destinations, were discussed. Only Bob and Harriet had booked already. They were booked to go on a cruise taking them through the Suez Canal. Then, not long afterwards, they were to go on a cruise through the Panama Canal. If they fulfilled their plans, Harriet would have achieved her ambition of sailing through most of the world's best known canals.

Harriet confirmed that the last few years had been busy travelling ones for them, following their dreams while they could. Their children were well-established, their bungalow and garden was small, easily looked after by family and neighbours in their absence. This led the Robinsons to state that their situation was similar, although he did worry, at times, about his three vintage cars, all Morgans. It was only to be expected that he would claim to have negotiated great deals on the purchase of each, on which he elaborated. His wheeling and dealing skills were hard to dispute from what he let drop in conversations, always adding his favourite phrase 'his success was enough on which to get by'.

There was a serious discussion about cars and also about the use of one's money in old age, so not all the chat could be called idle, or light-hearted. The two ladies, however, had disappeared and so their assumption of empty talk would not be truly accurate, not that their opinion mattered as Patsy had concluded earlier.

It was the first time that they had lunched together, with staff at The Kilimanjaro quickly obliging by putting tables together to accommodate the ten. No wonder the Robinsons were somewhat rotund, Jenny thought guiltily in noticing their helpings from the buffet were somewhat large. Nevertheless, they were an amenable couple, very content with their lot in life.

Paula Fowler, who was sitting opposite Jenny, was studying her hard, but it was Harriet who challenged her to reveal her thoughts. When she said they all agreed with what she had concluded on first meeting with Jenny, all stopped talking to await what she would go on to say. With all eyes upon her, blushing, Jenny joked that she was very sensitive and feared the verdict.

Undaunted, Paula went on to give the group's conclusion which was as follows: comfortable background, educated in a private school which the voice gave away. Lee had confirmed she was academically well qualified. It was Patsy who then continued.

"Large house and garden, with a man who does outside and a lady who does indoors."

"Moi," she said laughingly, but was taken aback that they were so close, and unnerved that she was so transparent. Except to say she was widowed, she had avoided answering any probing questions during the week of the group's stay, and Paula, as well as Patsy, had tried their best. Not that she had anything to hide but the intensity of curiosity was such that it caused Jenny, from devilment, to keep them guessing. There was fun in being intriguing.

Delroy assured Jenny that they all liked her and had considered her one of the group, and in no way a snob. Her thanks for that were drowned in the realisation of the time, almost two o'clock. This brought everything to a sudden halt. Their transport to the airport was to arrive at 2.30 p.m. They emphasised that it was Jacinta, and not Tanya, who had made the arrangement for them.

While all disappeared to their rooms to collect hand luggage, Jenny sauntered to the main entrance and took a seat on the verandah outside until it was time to say final goodbyes. Each in turn, cautioned her to take care which brought tears on seeing the minibus depart. Jenny knew she would miss them.

To revive her spirits and satisfy her curiosity, Jenny set off in the direction of 'El Viejo y El Mer'. The black limousine would not be there, of that she was sure, but it would be interesting to see whether the blue suited door men were on duty, or if they had only been there for the special visitor? By what she could see, the latter was the case. Even if there had been someone around to whom she might have made a casual remark about her last visit, the chance of having her curiosity satisfied, she guessed, would not have been high. So the mystery remained. However, the very bad section of road surface nearby had been re-tarred – coincidence or due to the visitor's influence, she would never know!

On this occasion, she did walk to the water's edge but stayed only briefly. The sound of the sea lapping at the shore put her in too much of a reflective mood. There was little opportunity for retail therapy, although, on the way back, Jenny looked around the small boutique near to the small supermarket, and then again at the one within the complex. Both offered swimwear, T-shirts, shorts, hats, lotions, with the former stocking sandals and belts. There was nothing to tempt her, so she came away empty handed. Still, from what she had observed, the Cubans were not fashion conscious. Most did not have the money, and the opportunities to tempt were not generally there.

From what she had read the Tiende Panamericanas and the Harris Bros store in Havana were well stocked and briefly Jenny toyed with the idea of going into Havana in search of these establishments. There was nothing she specifically wanted and just browsing never did appeal, so the notion was quickly dismissed. A quiet, relaxing time until she departed would not go amiss, her health had suffered several setbacks since Peter's death, her stamina had run low.

Back at the hotel, she had returned to her room to collect a book to read whilst she enjoyed a coffee in the foyer area, which was cool and quiet unlike the pool bar which was extremely busy. Her solitude, however, was short lived.

"Senora Moran, I have been looking for you."

Without looking up, she knew who had spoken. "Senor Rivero, I thought you were back in Mexico."

"Please, I join you," he said, sitting down.

Having presumed an affirmative response, she reacted tersely. "In Europe, it is rude for a gentleman to sit with his hat on when talking to a lady."

"I no want to make you angry, my beautiful Jenny."

Without his hat, his face seemed less rugged, mellowed by his greying, wavy hair. The smile, the eyes, all made for an attractive man. No bad catch for someone, Jenny thought, being sure that back in Mexico, many women would be eager for the well-heeled widower's attention.

The clothes he wore, his shoes, watch and fedora were not cheap, or casual. At the same time, Jenny reminded herself that the best conmen were always very well dressed, charming and suave, such facades hiding their sinister nature as in Rik's case. This caused her to shiver.

"Someone walking over my grave," she remarked, not that Vidal understood.

What he was eager to ask was whether Jenny would join him for dinner away from the marina, or could they dine together at the hotel if she did not want to venture elsewhere. The prospect of company was attractive and so she agreed, adding that she had a table booked for 7 p.m. at The Portofino. Her agreement pleased him greatly and, for the next half hour, they sat chatting in a mixture of Spanish and English. When she got up to leave, he got her to promise she would meet him at the lobby bar at 6.30 p.m. for a pre-dinner drink.

Back in her room, she began to regret saying 'yes'. On the positive side, it would be company, she would improve her Spanish though she would have to remember her dictionary. Her thoughts then turned to her earlier companions, wondering whether, or not, they would encounter any delay in their flight departure. Then, Jenny reflected on the holiday which had been so full of surprises. Dining with Vidal was something else to add to the list.

He awaited her, changed into his all-white attire which did not clash with Jenny's smart turquoise and fawn outfit – a fact which Vidal quickly pointed out. The small bar area was occupied by two of the Venezuelans with whom nods of recognition were exchanged. In fact, they became quite interested in watching, and no doubt, listening to the ensuing conversation between Jenny and Vidal.

Most of the chat centred around Rodrigo, following Jenny's inquiry as to his whereabouts. Without hesitation, she was told he had flown to Panama to meet up with Maria whose mother had just undergone an appendix operation. Maria's family were also hoteliers. It was Rodrigo's ambition to establish a hotel in Cuba, and it was an investigation into the prospects of this plan, not just the tourism conference, which had brought them to the island.

Rodrigo and Maria suited each other well, he explained. They complemented each other in their aims and ambitions. Rodrigo was good with figures, technology, negotiating while Maria charmed people at all levels, knew what would work, or would not. Vidal quite enthused about them both and was confident they would achieve a lot. It surprised her how freely he opened up and that his English was better than he had admitted previously. Certainly better than her Spanish.

Another yacht was coming in when they were walking to the restaurant and they stopped to watch it glide smoothly to its moorings.

"You like boats, you want best, then you come to Mexico and I'll buy you one."

"I should expect no less," Jenny laughingly responded, feeling a little make believe harmed no one.

Talk during the meal was about Mexico with Vidal, quite naturally extolling his country's virtues while Jenny pointed out the negatives, the drugs, the gangs, the crime and violence. This was done more to tease than to promote serious discussion. His response to her comments was:

"You come and see Mexico and you will love."

Jenny asked about the music and the 'cantinas' which led to talk of impromptu parties, musicians playing well into the night and people dancing. Things, she was assured she would love. The Mexicans, like the Cubans, had that feel for music and romance in their souls. By the passion with which this was expressed, she did not doubt it at all.

When they left The Portofino, people were beginning to gather in the nearby theatre area, ready for the show. Jenny said she was going to join the waiting audience to give support to the performers, some of whom were peeping out from their dressing area counting numbers. Without comment, he pointed to seats and both took their places. Music started to blare, a little loudly from the loud speakers, making any talk virtually impossible.

The fanfare of sound brought the resident musicians down from The Kilimanjaro and it was soon clear they had some vested interest in the troupe which was about to perform. There were several announcements that the show was about to begin, intended to hurry the late diners to join. Eventually, when the audience numbered around seventy or more, the cabaret began. There were eight dancers, one of whom looked anorexic, she was so thin. Nevertheless, her performance could not be faulted.

All involved threw their heart and soul into the

routines and the changes of costume were to be applauded. Vibrant in colour, looking clean and fresh, not easy considering the peripatetic life of such a troupe appearing at different hotels each evening. The older singer, in his forties, had a very good voice and knew his forte to be romantic ballads.

Never a fan of fire-eating, sword swallowing, or seeing someone lie on a bed of nails with another person standing on them, these performances made Jenny flinch which brought an inquiry of concern from Vidal. Again, when they were leaving at the end of the show, he put a hand on her shoulder to ask if she was alright. Then catching her unawares, he took hold of her hand.

"Come, we go for a drink, before goodnight," Vidal said.

Except for six of the Venezuelans enjoying a late evening snack, the pool bar was quiet.

"Café Americano." Greeted Jenny, to which she nodded.

Vidal agreed to the same but that a dash of tequila be put in both.

A further three couples arrived to take in the evening's lovely balmy air. All decided to have some freshly made potato crisps with their beers which made Jenny guess they were Cubans.

The chat with Vidal was light-hearted with him trying to encourage Jenny to use her Spanish vocabulary to describe the show. Aware that everyone around was Spanish speaking, she was more than a little self-conscious and so tried to whisper her responses. To find one word, she had to resort to her dictionary. At the same time, she looked up 'cheating', ready for any teasing, but none came.

Vidal was studying her closely, which he had been doing for much of the evening. This greatly disconcerted Jenny but she said nothing. She did not want to open that door. Compliments embarrassed her, and there had been several voiced. Time, she thought, to get back to the sanctuary of her room.

Escorted to the stairwell, she felt uneasy but there was no need, her escort made no unwanted advances. He kissed her hand, hesitated then gave a kiss on both cheeks, before walking away uttering, as usual, "Hasta luego!"

CHAPTER 20

Another beautiful, sunny day greeted her on awakening and Jenny was pleased with herself that she had not spent the night reflecting and analysing. Her lovely Peter had been a fatalist, 'que sera, sera', a sound policy. To avoid later crowds, she hurried to have her morning swim before breakfast. The afternoon, she had been warned, would be especially busy, with a large work group expected. For Cubans, the Mother's Day weekend was a very celebratory one.

At 7.30 a.m., the restaurant was busier than she expected. Leaving a book at her usual table, surprisingly not occupied even though it provided the best view, she turned to go and make her selection at the buffet bars, only to bump into Vidal.

"I join you," he pronounced happily, adding a pleading, "please!" as an afterthought.

Soon she was smiling realising she had a shadow, both starting with a selection of fruit, followed by an omelette. They differed only in that he chose coffee, while Jenny had her own teabags which amused him.

Although there was no need, he explained that he had

a business, and then a lunch appointment with a Cuban government official, and a Mexican friend from the Embassy. If she wanted a lift to Havana, he was sure the car picking him up would provide one. When she politely declined, he seemed disappointed. Then, he went on to insist that they dine together again, that they had much to talk about and discuss.

"Nothing serious," she responded, but felt the meaning was lost.

There was so much about her that he seemed to know, such as the fact that after breakfast, she usually took a short walk. Consequently, when they were outside, he asked whether she was going to turn left or right. To the right was her reply, thinking that the complex was like a small village, not just in design, but that much was noticed and gossiped upon.

A distance of some hundred yards, after turning left, brought them to the end of the cul-de-sac. There, a right turn, following a path at the gable end of one of the apartment blocks, brought them to where the boats turned to exit from the canals of the marina to make their way out to sea. At that point, walkers had to turn back, or turn right to take the towpath, minding the ropes. The latter option was vetoed by the presence of six Pekinese enjoying their breakfast, or otherwise yapping. The six spoilt pets had the run of their owner's cruiser, while the doting couple who regarded the dogs as their children, occupied one of the holiday apartments. They waved a cheery thank you that the dogs had not been disturbed in their repast!

Any plan to excuse herself, and escape to her room, was thwarted when the room maid, looking down from the walkway, shouted, "Buenas dias" and that she was working in the room.

Vidal smiled and told Jenny she was meant to keep him company. The phrase was stressed, or so she thought before rebuking herself for reading into it more than was meant.

They wandered on before sitting at a table shaded by a large umbrella, just one of three in a small patio area by The Portofino, not often used. No prompting was needed for her to learn more about Vidal and his business. His parents were not rich, nor poor either. They owned land in Acapulco which he inherited as his brother died at the age of fifteen. In addition, he had inherited land from an uncle but, to gain capital, he had gone to the US to work long hours at a lot of jobs. On returning to Mexico, he had seen and married his Elena and they opened a small hotel, worked hard, and expanded.

Their hotel, he stressed, was always special, not ordinary, important people came to eat and to stay. They made money, but Elena was overwhelmed, out of her depth, not happy, as they moved up the social ladder. Yet, he emphasised, she was as good as, and equally as beautiful and intelligent as, the rich, important people they met. There was passion expressed, and even a tear hurriedly brushed away, with which she could empathise. It seemed appropriate to remind him of the time, his transport was due at ten o'clock.

Again declining the offer of a ride to Havana, she

agreed to meet him on his return. In the distance, as Vidal walked off, she saw Lee wave and indicate, by sign, they get together for coffee to which she gave a thumbs up. So, as not to immediately follow in Vidal's wake, she waited a few minutes only to hear her name and find the two ladies behind her. They were coming from breakfast, confessing to have overslept, causing them to miss the morning courtesy bus. In addition, they told her that taxis were expensive and queues for buses incredibly long.

Not wishing to be unkind, Jenny refrained from stating that she would have told them all this if they had not indicated any help, or advice, was not necessary. They were not so reticent in their observations. The company of Vidal was her business and she bit her tongue, indicating Lee was waiting for her, pointing that she was putting two cups of coffee down on a table for her and was waiting.

It was good to see Lee whom Jenny had not glimpsed for days, and had wondered if she had left. There were bruises on her arm which she presumed came about when the green suited Chinese gent had grabbed her. No reference was made to the incident even though reference was made to Jenny's compatriots. Lee, however, volunteered information about her recent absence spent in Varadero. Her Canadian travelling companion, Kim, had loved the sandy peninsula, and its holiday hotels, especially the hedonistic attitude, but Lee had hated every moment.

When the two were joined by Kim who mentioned seeing Mr Rivero leaving in a car driven by someone he clearly knew well, both eagerly awaited Jenny's reaction. The anticipationary silence was broken by Lee.

"She's not going to tell us anything," she mischievously sighed.

"Nothing to tell."

With that Jenny left them to their imagination, just like the two ladies, and made her way back to her room, and the sanctuary of the balcony. The two men aboard the yacht beneath did give a wave, something they had not done before. Thus, in settling down with her book, in the most sheltered corner, she did wonder what had occasioned the honour.

At one o'clock, Jenny decided a salad would not go amiss. Her usual table was again available although the Kilimanjaro was bustling. No doubt, the staff had kept other guests away. Helen, before leaving, had admitted that the way Jenny was treated irked her. At least, Jenny had saved her from being too annoyed by dining in The Portofino each evening where the staff were just as attentive, eager to know everything was to her liking. All this she attributed to PRO Rosa. Almost every day, by phone, or in person, she checked if all was well.

Around the pool was busy. There were children, only seen at weekends. Later, there were to be competitive games held for them in and around the children's pool area. Any music played during the day was usually quiet and relaxing. On that afternoon, a DJ announced the aim of keeping all awake. This would not have gone down well with any of the old crowd, whom she guessed would have arrived back at their homes.

While Jenny was momentarily lost in her thoughts, Lee appeared telling her that Kim had gone on the courtesy bus to Havana. The two ladies had gone, too, but very clearly they had upset Lee. All attempts to make polite conversation had failed and the impression given that 'empty headed' young women like Kim and Lee should be ignored. With that she excused herself stressing that she was going to her room to do some academic work. Laying the emphasis on the word academic.

Stirred into a decision, Jenny decided a comfortable seat in the coolness of the lobby, where coffee would be available, would serve well for the next hour or so. Late afternoon, there might be a chance to swim.

The lobby was deserted and she settled down to finish the hefty tome so it could be left behind. For over an hour, it remained very quiet. The sound of sudden activity was ignored until the under manager presented her with a neat posy of blue and white flowers in honour of Mother's Day. This was just one of the numerous posies the hotel had ordered for the occasion.

Embarrassed to be included, when Juan was called away to deal with something, she hastened to leave to put the flowers in water. Her timing could have been better.

"Senora Moran," the voice was unmistakeable.

Vidal was standing by a distinguished looking gentleman with a goatee beard, the beard not as grey as his hair. Did they use the same tailor, she wondered, noticing a similarity in outfits.

"Come, Jenny, I introduce you."

Vidal's attempt to give his full name and official title

was overruled.

"I'm Francis. It's a pleasure to have the opportunity to meet you. I can appreciate why Vidal was so anxious to get back. Especially now that I have seen you. I am even more disappointed that you both cannot join my family for dinner this evening. Some important matter to discuss, I gather. Such a pity."

His English was perfect, with only a slight hint of an accent. Somewhat taken aback by what he had said, Jenny responded as expected adding that her Cuban holiday had been full of surprises, now topped by meeting a Consul General, no less. She had noticed the diplomatic plates on the car near where they stood.

"Now remember," he said with a wink, "if you need help, I can pull strings. Regrettably, I must rush off. Very good to have met you."

Swiftly with a kind of military precision, he entered the car which sped off. Steering Jenny to empty seats on the verandah, Vidal anticipated what she was going to ask by stressing that they did have much to talk about. Without interruptions, or argument, she had to hear him out. No light-hearted, flippant retort, would have been appropriate even though she feared what might be said.

What he wanted was for Jenny to visit Mexico for a month, or longer, as soon as possible after returning home, where he appreciated she would have matters to which to attend. All arrangements for her Mexican visit would be his responsibility and he would fly to London to accompany her. The trip would allow him to show off his country while they got to know each other better. It would show that he could offer her comfort and security as well as his love. Circumstances made it necessary to rush his proposal. He trusted the answer would be yes, if only, in the meantime, to the trip with no strings attached.

Near tears, Jenny's immediate wish was for the ground to open up and swallow her. Her salvation came in the form of Juan seeking to speak with Senor Rivero. This allowed her to excuse herself and leave.

"I see you at 6.30," Vidal said, rising to his feet.

Upon hearing this, Juan suggested they met at the Piano Bar.

Even though there was never any possibility of her accepting either option, Jenny's thoughts were in a turmoil. In different circumstances a paid holiday to Mexico would be very appealing. What concerned her was how to say thank you, but no, in the kindest of ways? The whole situation might seem very unreal, the stuff of romantic novels, except that it was actually happening, which was her dilemma. The reality and the sincerity of it all was not in doubt. Only too well, she appreciated that people could hide dark secrets and their nasty natures. Rik van Huyten was just such an example and the world contained a whole host of men, with all sort of vices.

Over the years, many had remarked about her intuition, how uncannily correct it could be after just one meeting. From the evening she had met Vidal, Jenny had sensed the loneliness which had drawn him to seek her company. There with his son and daughter-in-law, seeing their loving relationship, would have enhanced his awareness of having no partner and, in a holiday environment, this would have been pronounced. From then on, clearly his infatuation had grown.

Yet, he was a businessman, and a successful one and to get on needed to be hard headed. It had been mentioned, she would be an asset? Such were her thoughts when she was greeted by Kim back from her brief visit to Havana. Lee had a 'Do Not Disturb' notice on her door, hearing which, Jenny suggested that it was because she was trying to do some 'academic' work. Kim, however, was not convinced. The visits of Mr Chan had upset Lee greatly and his anger stemmed from some disagreement regarding one of her husband's export deals, which was all Kim knew. Although she had never met Lee's husband, Kim had decided she did not like him and believed her friend deserved better.

Perhaps, with more time to chat, Jenny might have gleaned more despite the fact that it had been mentioned that Lee spoke little of life back in Shanghai. The other comment of note, Kim had made, was that Lee did not lack money and must be from China's 'nouveaux riches'.

Back in her room, she realised that she had forty minutes to get ready for the evening. Still that was time a plenty. To her surprise at 6.30 p.m., she found Vidal sitting in a buggie waiting for her to appear.

"How you say…?"

Jenny finished the sentence for him. "Madam's carriage awaits."

The porter, driving the vehicle, looked bemused as to why his services had been needed to take them but a short distance. Still, it helped to create some light banter and gave a glimpse of Vidal's sense of humour. Indeed as they climbed the stairs to the Piano Bar, the light-heartedness continued. When he said she was breathless at getting to the top of the flight, she replied:

"Descarado," hoping she had remembered the correct word for 'cheeky'.

The barman, after preparing two Tequila cocktails, left giving them complete privacy to talk. This was not necessary as Vidal quickly stated that if her answer was no, he did not want to hear it. A 'no' would mean she needed more time to think about the offer. In consequence, she said nothing in order to enjoy the evening. They sat, chatted, commented on the now empty pool, the few remaining day visitors having their last snack before departing. Jenny mentioned that Gus had played the piano when the room had been made available during the Carballos' surprise visit. Piano playing was not one of Vidal's talents, a guitar, he would have strummed.

Their arrival at The Portofino seemed to cause a stir of interest amongst the other diners. This Jenny attributed to Vidal's tan fedora which he had donned rather than carry. When in her company, he no longer kept it on, having noted her comment. According to Vidal, it was the beautiful, smartly dressed Jenny who had caused heads to turn.

Following the meal, they went to the theatre area to await the start of the evening's entertainment. The troupe was a different one, but again very enthusiastic in their performances. Four men and four girls performed dances from around the world to music played by a five-piece band.

During the many changes of costumes, two young male singers sang either solo or together, very melodious Latin American tunes. At the finale, the two main dancers sought partners from the audience and headed straight for Jenny and Vidal. A modern disco type dance had to be followed, which they did quite well. Then, the music changed to the inevitable salsa and others in the audience were invited to come and participate, and so a brief dancing session followed which everyone enjoyed.

Finally, over coffee, Jenny was able to say how flattered she had been by Vidal's attention, that she had enjoyed his company and was greatly touched by his offer and proposal. When back in Mexico, he would be very relieved she had not accepted. He disagreed and wanted her to think again overnight, or even when back home, dropping his card into her small bag which was on the table.

On getting back to her room on the dot of midnight, Jenny felt like a teenager having been given a goodnight kiss by a new beau. Vidal had surprised her, taking her into his arms and kissing her with quite a passion. A kiss, he had said, to help her decide to say 'yes'.

CHAPTER 21

When going to breakfast at seven o'clock, Jenny noticed that the pool had another early bird that morning, namely a gentleman who called out her name. It was not someone she recalled seeing before. The voice definitely sounded English. Swimming to the edge near to where she had stopped, he introduced himself as Alan Thompson. He and his wife, along with another English couple, had arrived the previous day.

Jenny guessed why he had her name. Tanya's role was not one she had sought but it had come her way by the said young lady's default. It reminded her that she had not been given any details with regard to her own departure. Not that it mattered in this instance, for Leon had arranged for Pedro to collect her at 3 p.m., drive her around Havana before proceeding to the airport, according to her flight time, and any known delay.

Alan Thompson asked if she could meet them for a coffee at around 10.30 a.m. to give them advice about the island. Then, at breakfast, it was not long before she was joined by Vidal who was to be leaving for the airport at 9.30 a.m. His presence, his smile, the look in his eyes, caused an inner stir of anger. Anger at the loss of Peter, his protection, and being on her own. Great memories were a comfort, but the underlying ache of loneliness persisted. There was also guilt at being flattered by the interest of another man.

Consequently, Jenny felt that she had gone through breakfast ritual like a zombie. There had been some light-heartedness as Vidal tried several ploys to get her to say the word 'Si'. However, she was determined not to be caught out answering 'no' to everything said, or asked. Yet, it was no game. In answer to Vidal's request, after breakfast, she sat with him at that hidden table by The Portofino. They had a laugh at something she attempted to say in Spanish, which she agreed was getting worst rather than better. There was poignancy in the retort that all that was needed was more practice.

When it was a few minutes after nine o'clock, she stood up to say her goodbye and hand over a letter she had written, including his card in the envelope. A quick escape was made impossible as he held her hand firmly. Goodbyes always made her emotional and this one was going to be very hard.

"Why you no say yes? You not meant to be alone and unhappy." He then kissed her gently on the lips, squeezed her hand, turned and walked away quickly towards reception.

With tears now flooding, Jenny ran to her room where she really began to sob. She could hear Peter's voice saying, as he had often done, 'There's never a dull moment when you're around'.

Things did happen to her, or around her. People were drawn to her, and it was said she could never go unnoticed. 'Once seen, never forgotten', whether said jokingly, or not, was a description she had never understood, or appreciated, and Rik had proven it to be quite incorrect.

All the tears in the world would not bring back her soul-mate, life had to be lived, and, pulling herself together, she decided she had time for a quick swim before meeting the Thompsons. There were five in the pool but they were talking, not swimming. In view of the number gathering around, however, the relative quietness would not last.

The Scottish ladies approached her to inquire if she had met the Thompsons and the other newly arrived couple. That was the very question she was asked again when she met the Thompsons as arranged, namely had the other couple been seen? The answer to that was no, not that she had any reason to be interested, or concerned. Out of goodwill, she did not mind passing on general and useful information which they were keen to hear. At the same time, she stressed that the Thompsons should seek to ensure Tanya did fulfil her responsibilities, but if not, Jacinta was there to help. Thus, they should introduce themselves to her the next day when she would be on duty.

Her task completed and her coffee finished, she excused herself only to find PRO Rosa waiting to speak to her suggesting the reception might allow a quieter place. Her immediate two topics were predictable: was

Jenny happy with no complaints? The other was Tanya, and her shortcomings.

On reaching her desk, Rosa gave Jenny a small posy of flowers similar to that given to her previously, again, it was to note it was Mothering Sunday. Following this, an envelope and small package was handed over, with Rosa eagerly urging her to open them, suggesting the package first. Inside, she found a lovely gold bracelet with small amethysts inlaid in it. Rosa gasped, while Jenny felt shocked, shaken and tearful again. Her hands were shaking in opening the envelope and reading the note it contained. Tears clouded her eyes, and then began to stream. In Spanish, the note said:

'Remember me always, Lovely Jenny
Your Vidal'.

The blood drained, dazed, speechless, she failed to prevent Rosa putting the bracelet on her wrist with expressions of admiration. These drew the attention of some others, including the two Scottish ladies who claimed they had been looking for Jenny wanting to tell her they were going on a two-day trip and would not see her the next morning.

The ladies were told the bracelet was a gift from the Carballos whom they might have glimpsed during their visit on the evening they had arrived. Not for a moment did she think they accepted the story and fully expected some gossip.

"It has to be sent back," Jenny muttered to Rosa,

when they were alone again.

"Not possible, and very unkind," Rosa whispered before moving away to answer the phone.

At lunch, she was joined by the Thompsons whose attention was quickly drawn to the bracelet which Jenny had failed to unclasp. The interest of the two ladies continued, choosing a neighbouring table, no doubt, agog to glean any further information from any chance remark. Even the elusive Lee managed to be at her side as she selected from the buffet, drawing the attention of Kim to the piece of jewellery.

"Jenny get this from an admirer, expensive," she said with a grin and loudly enough to draw the attention of anyone who understood English. Then, like a mischievous fairy, she bounced away giggling. Before following, Kim added:

"Mr Rivero has very good taste."

A quiet afternoon on the balcony seemed the best option to Jenny noticing a somewhat carnival atmosphere around the pool. The need to relax quietly was compelling. The last two weeks, and especially the last couple of days had been quite emotional, events had been so unexpected. Life had not been dull and memories of this holiday would be different.

Suitably revived, feeling her positive self again, Jenny thought a cup of tea would be nice. In exiting her room, she noticed a note had been pushed under her door. It was an invitation to a farewell drink with management at the Piano Bar, to which Rosa had added the postscript that there would be no surprises. Thus, she guessed it would be Juan and Rosa. She was sorry Jacinta was not on duty to be able join them.

The idea of tea was abandoned as all around was busy, a walk seemed a better alternative, it would be her last opportunity. Della, the masseuse, was seeing off a client and came over to Jenny eager to look at the bracelet. In doing so, she reminded Jenny of what she had said, adding that she had seen a gift and knew that the offer of travel would be rejected, but had said nothing in order not to exert any influence.

"You need big hug." Then kissing Jenny on both cheeks, she whispered, "Always wear bracelet." This said, Della turned to attend to her next client who had just approached the salon.

What else had Della envisaged, Jenny wondered, during her walk towards the sea. The fear of hearing something unsettling always made her shy away from horoscopes and looking into the future, but she had an open mind on the subject. Her immediate concern was limited to the morrow, the flight back, that it would go well and smoothly, and no missing luggage.

Later, when she arrived at the Piano Bar, Juan and Rosa were there waiting. Did she owe this invitation to Vidal? Nothing was said except that Mr Rivero was a very nice gentleman who clearly thought highly of Jenny, who did seem to have important friends. No other observation was made, acknowledging Jenny's lack of comment and change of subject. Instead, she mentioned how much she had enjoyed her visit to Cuba. The people were friendly, warm and genuine. With regard to the island's future, she trusted that there would be peaceful change. On this, they were not to be drawn. Still, the general chat was interesting and flowed freely that three quarters of an hour passed quickly.

Once again, the Portofino was busy with much to observe. Whilst enjoying her meal, she reflected positively on her Cuban experience and wished her Spanish was much better. In her bag, was her valuable companion, a Spanish-English dictionary. Someone had mentioned to her, way back, that a hundred words was all you needed in a language to get by. This seemed very few.

It had been Jenny's intention to collect a book to read before going for coffee, that is, until she heard Lee's unmistakeable voice calling her name. It came from across the pool, where she could see Lee beckoning her over. The bracelet continued to be of interest, with a group of Venezuelans being drawn into the admiration society. By now, Jenny was resigned that everyone, no doubt, knew from whom she had received this generous gift. What other thoughts some might have, she dreaded to think.

From Kim, she learnt that the other English couple had been seen. In addition, she gathered that their three weeks in Cuba ended a day after Jenny's departure. Lee had a further three months in Toronto, before returning to Shanghai, and a husband she had not seen for twelve months. While Lee assured Jenny that she had been true to him, Kim voiced uncertainty over whether the husband would have been so loyal.

Jenny sought to turn the conversation to Chinese communities worldwide, making reference to the Chinatown in Toronto. This was done in the hope it might lead to the mention of a certain green suited visitor but her curiosity was not rewarded. Away from home, Lee did not want to be with other Chinese.

"Other people more interesting, other music nicer."

Even the Venezuelans joined Lee in expressing disappointment that there were no musicians to serenade them.

Despite being urged to linger longer, soon after eleven, Jenny said goodnight, determined to be in bed before midnight. The following day would be long, and usually she did not manage to sleep for long on overnight flights.

CHAPTER 22

Waking on the dot of 6 a.m., Jenny cast aside any thought of lingering in bed, deciding instead to stick to her morning routine. Any tiredness later would help her to sleep on the flight back to Paris. The cloud of volcanic ash over Spain, and other parts of Europe, was causing flight delays, and longer flight times.

All Jenny ever cared about were safe journeys whether by land, sea or air. The rampaging anger of some passengers over delays, witnessed over the years, she had never understood, although she would agree that airline staff should keep people regularly updated in such circumstances. Still, her immediate thoughts were to have an enjoyable, leisurely morning.

By 8.30 a.m., even her packing had been done. All that remained was to put in her bathing costume when dry, and the light dress she was wearing, when she changed into her travelling clothes. This, she intended to do just before going to lunch around one o'clock. To allow the room maid to carry out her duties, she decided it was a good time to return the pool towels and then seek Jacinta and Rosa for a farewell chat.

On leaving the room, Jenny stopped before reaching the stairs, sure she had heard a kind of sobbing groan. There was nothing to be seen, but approaching the walkway to a nearby room, the kind of sobbing noise got louder. Then she saw a woman, ghostly white in pallor, her long greying brown hair hanging limply around her distressed face, her dress clinging damply to her body.

Whatever the cause of the woman's agitation and sickly appearance, Jenny was in no doubt the immediate situation was serious. It was important to get her to sit down before she fell down. Her distraught state prevented her being able to speak and it was very clear she desperately wanted to say something. The brief description which had been given of the elusive English couple convinced Jenny that she had found the wife which would mean no language barrier.

It took a little persuading to get the frantic, shivering woman to sit on the floor with Jenny who was urging her to take deep breaths like herself. In this way the hyperventilating was controlled enough firstly for the words, "Help me! Help me!" to be uttered.

Slowly, between sobs, the problem was explained. The husband had collapsed and was on the floor groaning. Panic stricken, she had exited the room to shout for help. The door had closed and locked behind her leaving her helpless outside with not a sound to be heard from within.

To ensure that the true seriousness of the situation was appreciated at reception, Jenny decided to run the hundred and fifty yards or so there, rather than try to phone from the room, which also might not be hurriedly answered. Explaining to Jean her intention, and that she should remain seated until her return was difficult. There was fear of being abandoned and some random and strange suggestions stuttered.

Once out of Jean's hearing, and on the road towards reception, Jenny began running speedily, shouting, "Medico! Puede llamar un medico!"

No one from the crowds of people by two coaches responded.

At reception, in Spanish, then in English, she explained that a doctor was needed very urgently in Room 103.

"The man is unconscious, the woman is ill also. A key is needed to enter the room. Please doctor, nurse, key needed!"

Reaction to the news was immediate. Although confident the necessary help would arrive quickly, the complex had its own medical centre, Jenny still shouted for a doctor, a medico on her way back in case one of the increasing number of people around was so qualified. Jean was standing shakily but on seeing Jenny collapsed in a heap. Quickly Jenny put her in the recovery position and insisted she stayed in that position. Help, she emphasised, was just seconds away. Fortunately the all-important buggy was just arriving below. Frantically, Jenny waved from the walkway to ensure no time was wasted finding the room. Meeting the doctor and nurse at the top of the stairs, she told them all she knew.

While the door was being opened, the nurse turned

her attention to Jean. Luckily, both doctor and nurse spoke English fairly well. Before departing, Jenny was told Jean's husband had suffered a very serious seizure. The fear was that giving Jean the news, and seeing him, would induce a heart attack, which later was exactly what happened.

Wearily making her way towards the reception again, Jenny was greeted near the pool bar, by a smart gentleman offering her a coffee, which was just what she needed her throat felt so dry.

"I think you are in need of this. Please sit. Are you sure you are alright?"

He had a lovely lilting accented voice and, feeling a little cold, Jenny guessed her lack of colour explained his concern.

"Thank you, I'm fine, breathless perhaps."

Further conversation was interrupted by the Thompsons who had seen Jenny on her return sprint and were curious. Their impression of the Davidsons was that, although not old, they had not seemed the most robust of couples. In fact, they had wondered why they had chosen such a long haul destination. Thus, without hesitation, on hearing the sad news, they assumed the travelling to have been the cause, the deep vein thrombosis, in this instance, happening in Mr Davidson's brain.

Their speculation, probably, was correct, but Jenny was not going to enter into any conjecture. At this point, her main concern was to ensure that Tanya was made aware of the situation and got to the hospital quickly.

Whilst talking to the Thompsons, two ambulances had arrived and then departed with lights flashing.

To Jenny, it was reassuring that the poorly couple had received medical help within that 'vital golden hour'. At reception, she found Jacinta and Rosa busily seeking to contact Tanya. Almost in chorus, both wanted to be assured Jenny was all right. People's concern was touching but also a little baffling until she thought about the situation which had faced her. Some would have flustered and worsened the problem, but she knew she acted well in a crisis. If she began to recall those concerning Peter's health in the two years before his death, she would be in a flood of tears.

The sanctuary of her room had to wait, Lee and Kim stopped her retreat insistent that she needed company and a drink after such a shock, and having saved two people. Stunned that they should have heard any tale, let alone such an exaggerated one, so quickly, Jenny quietly succumbed.

Long before this, she had decided that the complex was truly like a village where nothing went unnoticed, or commented upon. The two, however, did not interrogate her for details but chatted about other subjects, clearly having taken it upon themselves to take Jenny's mind off the early morning events – events she could not have foreseen, or chosen in any way in which to be involved.

It was 12.30 p.m. when Jenny returned to her room to change and finish her packing. A quiet leisurely lunch would be her oasis of calm before later facing the bustle of the airport. Her wish was granted and having lingered, the remaining time before she was picked up by Pedro soon passed, especially as much of it was taken up by a surprise visit from Tanya, who had been unaware she was due to leave!

At the hotel to get some of the Davidson's possessions, she wanted also to give Jenny an update. Mr Davidson was critically ill with his survival very much in the balance. Further tests were taking place to ascertain the state of Jean Davidson's heart after some mild cardiac episode.

Jenny's concern was that the very fragile state of Mrs Davidson was appreciated and that Tanya assured she was supported as much as possible. However, so that she could leave the hospital, Tanya had got a friend with good English to take her place.

"Mrs Davidson needs people to be with her night and day."

"Agreed. Jean Davidson is going to face some very difficult days in a hospital far from home, now knowing the language spoken."

"I have a rota ready for the next thirty-six hours."

A smile, and a look between the two women said a lot. Jenny acknowledged that Tanya was rising to the situation, and a task which was not easy, traumatic in fact. Tanya showed that she knew it was imperative she coped well.

"My job, important to me."

Pedro's arrival, and cheeky wink at Tanya, saw her depart towards Room 103 with a spring in her step, her spirits raised. In greeting Jenny, he was quick to let her know that he had checked with the airport if any flight delay was expected. The reply had been that the 20.20 Air France flight to Paris would not leave at the scheduled time; a delay of, at least, two hours was expected.

"No need to rush."

"Even so, let's get to the airport no later than 6 o'clock."

"Mrs Moran, why are you in such a hurry to leave the lovely island of Cuba?"

A reason might have been suggested, only a glance from Jenny made him reconsider.

It was soon obvious that Pedro had thought carefully about the route which would be taken. From the Malecon (seafront) he turned to Calle 23, or La Rampa, the city of Havana's business centre. Then, turning off, he drove towards the Mueso Napoleonica which he considered was overlooked by tourists. Yet, as was pointed out, it housed a remarkable collection of Napoleonic memorabilia in an island with no connection with the French Emperor. All had been amassed by a rich individual, clearly with great interest in Napoleon Bonaparte.

Next he drove to the Cementario de Cristobal Colon where Jenny got out briefly to view this 'city of the dead' with its massive marble mausoleums. A very stooped, elderly lady carrying flowers passed by and it was said that, most likely, she was going to pray to 'La Milagrosa', the miracle worker, helper of people in need. Both hoped the woman's prayers would be answered. There was a tranquillity and a haunting attraction about the place.

From the cemetery, Pedro detoured to pass the National Theatre and to give Jenny a chance to see again the Plaza de la Revolución. The vast square was empty except for four people standing near the middle of the vast concourse idly looking around. The emptiness made it look like a sterile waste of space. Clearly its only use was to house the masses on May Day, a place where Fidel Castro, in his heyday, could regale the people. Pedro remarked that he had attended only once, with his parents, adding the family was not political.

After this there was not a great deal of chat on the drive towards the airport. The road was busy and concentration was necessary, as the driving of some was erratic. Just before arriving, Jenny had thanked Pedro for his services and wished him well for the future, that he achieved his dreams. Responding he assured her that Mr Carballo had set him on his way.

Spying the information desk on entering the departure building, Jenny headed briskly towards it, her case in tow, the people milling around making it an obstacle course. The appropriate queue was not far away, or over long. A short middle-aged woman with titian coloured hair, who seemed to have followed her from the entrance, seemed eager to talk even though her English was limited.

From Paris, her German speaking fellow passenger would be flying on to Zurich. The delay irked her but Jenny surmised that this was mainly because she was a nervous flier. When both sought to purchase their departure tax voucher, and were jostled by a group of exuberant, young Russians, her seemingly timid, new acquaintance loudly uttered:

"Russians, I not like," adding a spiel of German, or it could have been Russian. It silenced the group and allowed her to get to the front, pulling a startled Jenny along with her.

Once through passport control and the security checks, her Swiss fellow traveller, indicated she was going to sit and read, showing a bulky tome. Jenny decided to view duty free, only to find there several Russian couples on a buying spree. In fact, as time passed, she concluded that all the Russian passengers had done likewise and that too many had consoled themselves during the ever increasing delay in indulging in the local beverage – rum.

The clinking of bottles was very noticeable when, finally at 23.45, people on the flight to Moscow were called to board. Rounding up eight wayward, somewhat 'happy' Russians, further delayed boarding for the Paris flight, a fact not well accepted by many tired, and peevish, after a very long period of waiting. Even the minutes taken up by the police escorting a tall, Englishman in his late fifties, once good looking but whose features now bore witness to a life lived hard, riled the throng. A further police escort awaited in Paris to escort the miscreant to his onward flight to London.

In the queue to board, Jenny found herself again standing by the Swiss lady, agitated and very eager to be on her way. That they were not to be sitting together disappointed, a presumption no doubt made as they had checked in at the same time.

When, at last, forty-five minutes past midnight, the plane took off, there seemed to be a collective sigh of relief. Less than half an hour afterwards, the calm for Jenny and others sitting nearby, was broken when a woman, in the aisle seat in front of her became ill. Calls were made for doctors resulting in five responding to the appeal. Clearly, not all were needed.

The woman needed oxygen and her falling blood pressure became a concern. Things happen in threes, but the thought of another patient in her vicinity was more than Jenny wanted. The offer of a seat elsewhere was welcomed particularly as the woman's condition would have to be monitored so there would be constant activity near to her seat.

Jenny's new seat, near to the rear of the plane, was between a young Croatian student and a tall hurdler from a Cuban athletic team whose slumber she had disturbed. It did not take long for him to resume his sleep and as no turbulence was encountered, Jenny also managed several much needed naps. One of the crew was heard to remark later that everyone had been especially quiet and sleepy.

To avoid the volcanic cloud hanging over Spain, the route to Paris had included quite a detour, making the flight time twelve hours, and not ten. The 17.30 touchdown time in Paris left Jenny no time to idle, following security checks, to change terminals and catch the 18.30 flight to Manchester. The tail end of the queue was disappearing when she reached the gate. Once on board and seated, the plane was moving determined to ensure its scheduled slot.

The businessman beside her was pleasant and chatty, glad of her company being another not enamoured at flying, even though his job necessitated much more than he wanted. Consequently, he had decided to seek a sideways move with a salary cut. This step was being taken to allow time with the family which all the travelling greatly restricted.

The fact that Jenny had gone on holiday to Cuba on her own, earned the comment, "Gutsy."

"Perhaps you are too polite to say 'foolhardy' but I had done my homework before going and knew I would not feel threatened in any way."

This led to a discussion about the island and some speculation as regards its political and economic future.

When they disembarked, courteously, he insisted on carrying her hand luggage, a small bag but heavy, all the way through to baggage reclaim. It warmed her to end her holiday on such a positive note, that gallantry was not dead.

By 7.45 p.m. she was back at the airport hotel and unlike when she left, the place was extremely busy. Jenny was lucky to get a booking for dinner at 8.15 p.m. Time, she concluded, for a quick shower before an enjoyable, leisurely dinner, and then bed. Those were Jenny's intentions, praying for no untoward incident, or unexpected excitement.

CHAPTER 23

On the Wednesday morning, not long after 9 a.m., Jenny began her drive home. There was no rush, but she knew it would be good to get that sadness at returning alone, to an empty house, over with early, rather than later in the day. Undoubtedly too, there would be messages to attend to, though the accumulation of post would not arrive from Keepsafe until the following day.

The weather began cold, gloomy with a hint of dampness. Then, as the journey progressed, changed to cloudy and bright interrupted by the occasional heavy shower. Except to recall the sun and the warmth, she had enjoyed the last fortnight, Jenny gave no real thought to her holiday, or to that unhappy issue it had raised.

During the flight back, she had resolved to 'let it go' and not let it trouble her, for that would be futile. In any case, the traffic was heavy and included lots of large lorries, some trundling slowly, others speeding to the limit, so full concentration was vital.

Nearing journey's end, she detoured in order to shop for fruit and salad ingredients. Thus, a part of normal routine had started even before arriving back, showing